The ties that bind may be the ties that kill, as these extraordinary women race against time to beat the genetic time bomb that is their birthright....

Lynn White:

With enhanced senses, and super speed and strength, this retrieval specialist can breach any security—but has she been working for the wrong side?
DECEIVED by Carla Cassidy—January 2005

Faith Corbett:

This powerful psychic's secret talent could make her the target of a serial killer— and a prime suspect for murder.
CONTACT by Evelyn Vaughn—February 2005

Dawn O'Shaughnessy:

Her superhealing abilities make her nearly invincible, but can she heal the internal wounds from years of deception?
PAYBACK by Harper Allen—March 2005

* * *

ATHENA FORCE: The adventure continues with three secret sisters, three unusual talents and one unthinkable legacy....

Dear Reader,

What do you plan to accomplish in 2005? Let Silhouette Bombshell jump-start your year with this month's fast-paced lineup of stories featuring amazing women who will entertain you, energize you and inspire you to get out there and get things done!

Author Nancy Bartholomew brings on the heat with *Stella, Get Your Man*. P.I. Stella Valocchi is on a missing-persons case—but with a lying client, a drug lord gunning for her and a new partner who thinks he's the boss, Stella's got her hands full staying cool under fire.

The pressure rises as our popular twelve-book ATHENA FORCE continuity series continues with *Deceived,* by Carla Cassidy, in which a computer whiz with special, supersecret talents discovers that she's on the FBI's Most Wanted list and her entire life may be a lie.

Reality isn't what it seems in the mystic thriller *Always Look Twice* by Sheri WhiteFeather. Heroine Olivia Whirlwind has a unique gift, but delving into the minds of crime victims will bring her ever closer to a ruthless killer and will make everyone a suspect—including those she loves.

And finally, travel to Romania with Crystal Green's *The Huntress,* as an heiress with an attitude becomes a vampire hunter on a mission for vengeance after her lover is captured by those mysterious creatures of the night.

Enjoy all four, and when you're finished, please send your comments to me c/o Silhouette Books, 233 Broadway, Suite 1001, New York, NY 10279.

Sincerely,

Natashya Wilson
Associate Senior Editor, Silhouette Bombshell

Please address questions and book requests to:
Silhouette Reader Service
U.S.: 3010 Walden Ave., P.O. Box 1325, Buffalo, NY 14269
Canadian: P.O. Box 609, Fort Erie, Ont. L2A 5X3

CARLA CASSIDY

DECEIVED

Published by Silhouette Books

America's Publisher of Contemporary Romance

Special thanks and acknowledgment are given to Carla Cassidy for her contribution to the ATHENA FORCE series.

 SILHOUETTE BOOKS

ISBN 0-373-51340-2

DECEIVED

CARLA CASSIDY

isn't a secret agent or martial arts expert, but she does consider herself a Bombshell kind of woman. She lives a life of love and adventure in the Midwest with her husband, Frank, and has written over fifty books for Silhouette.

Chapter 1

The rock glittered brilliantly against the swatch of navy velvet, a sparkling gem beneath a single spotlight in the glass display case. Fifteen carats of multifaceted perfection that threatened to steal Lynnette White's breath away...if she was breathing.

At the moment she was holding her breath and inching down a rope suspended from the large skylight overhead. She paused just before touching the display case and tilted her head to the right.

From the upstairs she could hear the sounds of the owner of the mansion snoring in his bedroom. Good. She'd gotten past the security guards outside the huge

mansion and had managed to breach the electronic security system to get inside. The last thing she wanted
was for the owner of the house to stumble downstairs
for a drink of water and discover her hanging like a
spider directly over his precious gem.

If she were like normal people she would never
have been able to hear the faint snores coming from
an upstairs bedroom. But Lynn wasn't normal people.

She looked at her watch, still listening for any
sound of movement inside the home. She knew the
owner was an elderly, eccentric millionaire who lived
alone. She hoped he hadn't chosen this night to invite
some lady friend to overnight hospitality. His household staff didn't live in the house, but were day workers who left after dinnertime.

She checked her watch again. Ten seconds and
there would be a thirty-second blip to the computer
security system. She'd hacked into the security files
and had programmed a fifteen-second delay that
hopefully wouldn't be detected during or after the
fact.

Thirty seconds was all she'd have to cut the top of
the glass display case, pluck up the gem and get the
heck out of Dodge. It shouldn't be a problem.

The smell of the house surrounded her, a scent of
lemon polish and the lingering smell of Italian cook-
ing that must have been dinner for the occupant.

She drew three deep, measured breaths as she

stared at the second hand on her watch. When it read precisely 1:00 a.m., she efficiently cut the glass, pulled out the circle with a piece of duct tape, then reached into the top of the display cabinet. She grabbed the cool diamond and placed it into the pouch in her spandex top, then climbed up the rope at warp speed.

Her heart hammered as she listened for the sound of an alarm or racing footsteps. But there was nothing except the pounding of her heartbeat and the faint sound of her own measured breaths.

When she reached the outside of the roof of the three-story stone house she yanked the rope up and coiled it over her shoulder. She carefully placed the panel of the skylight back where it belonged, then headed for the edge of the tiled roof.

A peek over the side of the building would have forced most people backward, away from the steep, sheer drop to the brick patio below. But the height didn't frighten Lynn. She'd come up the side of the building relatively easily, going down should prove no real problem.

She had no idea how long it would be before somebody would realize the prized diamond named the Star of Russia was gone. She hoped nobody would notice until morning but was aware that she might only have minutes or mere seconds to escape.

Heart still beating a frantic tattoo, she moved to the

downspout that had aided her climb up the side of the building. Checking to make sure the security guards were no place in sight, she began her descent.

Like a spider she used both the downspout and the uneven stones of the facade to make her way down the side of the building.

When she hit the patio she ran like the wind, across the lush grass lawn. The dark July night embraced her, shielding her from sight.

Euphoria washed over her as she raced to the place where her car was hidden in a copse of trees in a nearby public park.

She'd done it!

Granted, it had been an easier job than some of the others she'd pulled off. But she still felt that burst of confidence and competence that filled her after every successful heist.

She pulled the black stocking hat off her head as she ran, allowing her shoulder-length, chestnut hair to fall free. She knew she was taking a chance if anyone saw her and could describe her, but if she was seen she'd look more suspicious wearing a stocking cap at this time of year.

The car was where she'd left it, the sleek muscle car her uncle Jonas had disapproved of but that Lynn had been adamant about owning. Three months ago, in a rare burst of stubbornness, she'd fought him tooth and nail until he'd given in and let her buy the bright red Mustang. Before that time she'd been driven by a chauffeur wherever she needed to go.

In the car with its slick contours and powerful V-8 engine was the one place where Lynn felt free…completely liberated from the constraints and worries of her everyday life.

No sirens chased her down the coastal road to the south of Miami as she headed for the mansion she called home. Although she longed to open up the engine and fly with the windows down and the air smelling of midsummer and ocean, she heeded the speed limit.

She wasn't about to allow a speeding ticket to bust her now. Still, even driving the speed limit with her window rolled down, she felt that aura of freedom, of a world with no threat, of joy in the sheer pleasure of being alone. Jonas allowed her to be alone so rarely.

Smiling, her thoughts turned to the man who wasn't really her uncle but rather her godfather, the man who had raised her in the lap of luxury but with a paranoia and an isolation that had kept her feeling like the fairy-tale character Rapunzel most of the time.

Jonas didn't keep her in a tower, but she'd spent her youth surrounded by bodyguards, homeschooled through high school and isolated from her peers. She hadn't questioned her lifestyle until recently, when she'd begun to feel an edgy restlessness, the need for something different.

She touched the diamond that nestled close to her heart. Jonas would be proud. He hadn't known she was going after it tonight. She hadn't told him her plans. It was safer that way…both for him and for herself.

It took Lynn thirty minutes to reach the gates of her home. She punched in the code on her remote, and the iron gates parted to reveal the luxurious oceanside mansion where she lived with Arturo and Rita Batista, Cuban refugees who worked for her godfather.

Jonas was rarely in residence, having business interests all around the world. Although Jonas enjoyed enormous success in his import/export business and defense contract work, his real love was the work he and Lynn did covertly for the U.S. Government.

She parked her car in the garage, then entered the house through a mudroom just off the kitchen. She moved with the stealth of a cat, noiselessly through the massive kitchen and living room. As she moved, she listened for any sound that would indicate somebody had heard her car arrive.

The security guards stationed around the grounds and on the roof would have seen her arrive home, but they would think nothing of it. They were paid a lot of money for keeping their silence concerning the comings and goings of the occupants of the house, but to be completely safe, Lynn went on random night drives all the time. Most of the guards knew she suffered from insomnia and her near-nightly drives helped her relax.

As she made her way through the kitchen and across the living-room floor she was aware of the tiny blinking lights in the walls that followed her progress. They were sensor lights programmed specifically to her and Jonas.

If she spent more than five minutes in any room the temperature would adjust for her comfort level and the artwork on the walls would change to her personal favorite pieces. The elaborate system was one of Jonas's toys.

She paused on the first step of the grand staircase. If she allowed it, she would hear every sound the house and its occupants made…the tick of clocks, the hum of electricity flowing through wires and the drip of a faucet in an upstairs bathroom. Heightened senses were a gift with which she'd been born. At times growing up, that particular gift had seemed more like a curse. What was loud music to some became an intolerable pain to her. She often smelled what other people couldn't, felt heat and cold more intensely than others. But she had learned to filter sensation and control her body's responses.

She focused on a particular area of the house, the area in the back of the house on the bottom floor where Arturo and Rita lived and slept.

From that place she could hear Arturo's deep, regu-

lar snoring. Good. She didn't want to awaken him or
Rita, who would be up before dawn to prepare for Jonas's homecoming. Besides, as far as they were concerned, she'd gone to her bedroom around ten and had
gone to sleep.

When she reached her private quarters, she went
through the sitting room and into the bedroom to the
canopied bed and pulled the diamond from her top.
She flung herself on the bed and set the diamond in
front of her on the purple-and-gold brocade spread.
The gem was nearly blinding in its beauty.

She turned it first one way then another, admiring
the light refraction of the utter perfection of the bril-
liant-cut fifteen-carat round stone.

The diamond had been in the possession of a
Miami businessman named Sebastian Tyler, but he
wasn't the rightful owner of the gem.

According to what Jonas had told her, the rightful
owner was a peasant woman in Russia whose ances-
tors had been wealthy and powerful friends of Peter
the Great. The diamond had been stolen and sold on
the black market to Sebastian Tyler.

The U.S. authorities had contacted Jonas to see if
he could help return the diamond to its Russian owner.
When he had told Lynn about it, she'd immediately
begun to research Sebastian Tyler's home to find the
soft security spot.

Lynn frowned as she tucked the diamond into a velvet pouch, then placed it in her nightstand. She had done this kind of work dozens of times in the past, but lately, questions niggled at her, questions only Jonas could answer.

Questions that, at the moment, would have to wait.

Still, this was the work she loved, the work that she and Jonas did together. Although they didn't rob from the rich and give to the poor, they did rob from the wrong and give to the right.

Throughout history, artifacts and treasures had been stolen from their rightful owners during wars and coups. Jonas researched the items and their rightful places, and Lynn did the actual recovery work.

She rose from the bed, stripped off her clothes and padded into the large bathroom. A moment later, standing beneath a hot spray of water, she tried to blank the night's activities out of her mind.

It took only minutes to wash off the stress and climb into a pink silk nightgown. Because her senses were so finely tuned, she particularly loved the way silk felt against her body.

She shut off her bedroom light, then went to her window. It would take a while for her to wind down enough to sleep. She needed to sleep as soon as possible. She had grad-school classes in the morning.

The moonlight floated down in luminous rays, and from this vantage point it illuminated the ocean waves that crashed against the cliff upon which the house sat.

It was a million-dollar view from a multi-million-dollar house.

She eyed her computer on a desk in the corner. She could download her e-mail or wander into a chat room, but she wasn't in the mood.

As the exhilaration of the night's heist seeped away, she was once again filled with a restless energy, a yearning for something—but she didn't know what.

Jonas would be home tomorrow. Maybe that would help dispel the odd sense of melancholy she'd been feeling lately. When Jonas was at home it was Christmas, Thanksgiving and New Year's all rolled into one. There were presents and laughter and the only sense of family she ever enjoyed.

Surely that would take away the edginess and the caged-in feelings she'd been suffering lately. With that reassuring thought in mind, she turned away from the window and crawled into bed.

"Dammit." Nick Barnes scowled at the e-mail he'd just received from his supervisor, indicating there had been another heist overnight. This time the take had been a priceless diamond from the private residence of one Sebastian Tyler.

Nick knew there would be no mention of the robbery in the papers. The FBI was keeping a lid on the spat of robberies similar to this latest.

The Bureau was certain that Jonas White was involved. The man had been under investigation for years for a variety of crimes, including the black-market sale of stolen antiquities and treasures. The FBI had recovered several of the stolen pieces, and each roundabout trail had led back to Jonas or his right-hand man, Richard Dunst. Unfortunately, the trails hadn't included solid evidence that would ensure a conviction. The evidence was all loosely circumstantial. Nick knew there would be no proof, no evidence pointing directly to the man's culpability this time either.

Jonas White was as slippery as an eel, as cunning as a fox and as wealthy as Midas. He had also been Nick's sole assignment for the past two years.

The man had been under FBI investigation for art and arms smuggling, drug trafficking and a multitude of other crimes for years, but there had never been enough evidence for an arrest.

Seven years ago as a hotshot, new, twenty-two-year-old FBI agent, Nick had gone undercover and had worked a variety of assignments. Then, two years ago, at the age of twenty-seven, he'd been hired as head of Jonas's security team. The plan was for Nick to work his way into Jonas's confidence and gain access to the details of the illegal activities.

Lately Jonas had taken more of an interest in Nick.

For the past six months Nick felt as if he just might be being groomed for something big…something that would get him into a place where he could get the goods on the man, gain the knowledge to bring Jonas down.

He jumped as his cell phone rang. He closed down his e-mail program, then reached for his cell phone in his pocket. The caller ID showed the calling number as private. He flipped it open and said hello.

"Have you read your e-mail this morning?" The deep voice belonged to Nick's supervisor and only contact while he was so deep undercover, Ray Graham.

"Yeah, I saw it. Unfortunately, Mark was out of the country last night." Mark was their code name for Jonas. "The e-mail you sent me was sketchy…anything left behind?"

"Nothing. Just like the others." Ray heaved a deep, audible sigh. "It's like a ghost got in and out when the security guards outside blinked their eyes. It's time, Nick…time to play Post Office."

"Got it."

Nick clicked off and leaned back in his chair. Post Office. He'd known it was coming. He left the table and walked over to the small desk next to the kitchen sink. From the top drawer he pulled out a manila folder.

He grabbed a fresh cup of coffee, then stepped out sliding doors to a tiny patio that overlooked the ocean. He sat at the small table in the shade of the overhead umbrella and for a moment simply sipped his coffee and watched the waves crash to shore.

He'd been renting this place for the past four years under the name of Walter Tyndale. There was only one person in the world who knew Nick had this small beach house, and that was Ray.

Although his family had cut Nick out of their lives years ago, he and his older brother, Anthony, had maintained strained, occasional contact with each other, but even Anthony didn't know about Nick's real work or this safe house.

This place was his escape, his sanity in the dangerous world he'd built with lie after lie as an undercover agent. And now he was about to complicate the situation with more lies.

He opened the file folder he'd brought outside and looked at the picture of the young woman contained within. Lynnette White...Jonas's goddaughter.

When Nick had first started working for Jonas two years before, Lynn had been a gangly twenty-year-old. There was nothing gangly about her at twenty-two. During the course of the past two years, Lynn had physically blossomed, developing curves where there had been none before.

Up until now Nick had had very little interaction with her. A pleasant nod, a brief hello was all they'd shared in the past. But the game was about to change. She might be the key to bringing down Jonas.

He stared at the photo. It had been taken with a long lens from quite a distance away, but the lab had worked its magic to give him a photo that appeared to have been taken mere feet from her.

She'd been captured just before getting into her car after one of her classes at the nearby college. Her shoulder-length chestnut-colored hair framed her pretty features and her green eyes sparkled with life. She was slender, but not without feminine curves.

The picture had been taken by another agent during the ordinary course of building an up-to-date dossier on Jonas. In truth Nick knew little about her other than she had been sheltered most of her life and was now a grad student in computer science at Florida International University.

He touched her face with the tip of his index finger, a flash of adrenaline spiking through him.

Even though Nick felt that he was on the verge of being invited into Jonas's confidence, he'd known his superiors were getting tired of waiting for something to happen where Nick's undercover job was concerned. He wasn't surprised that they wanted Nick to turn up the heat by targeting Lynn.

Yes, she just might be the ticket to the arrest and conviction of Jonas. All Nick had to do was seduce her—become her lover and her confidant. Not exactly the worst assignment he could draw.

He knew that part of the reason he'd been tapped

for this particular job was because he was young and was considered to be handsome and charming, when he wanted to be. He had a reputation for being a ladies' man. A reputation built on the fact that Nick had enjoyed the company of a variety of women.

He slid the photo back in the folder, finished his coffee, then reluctantly went inside and prepared to leave his little sanctuary. There wasn't much to do in preparation for leaving. He only managed to spend time here briefly and only when Jonas was out of town.

Officially Nick lived in a luxury apartment with closets filled with silk suits and Italian-leather shoes, all bought and paid for by Jonas, who was a generous employer.

Seducing the lovely Lynnette wouldn't be easy. Jonas guarded her as if she were a precious artifact that might shatter if out of his control. But Nick didn't get his reputation as a superagent by backing away from difficult situations.

The other thing Nick had to consider was that if he struck up a relationship with Lynn and it went bad, then it was quite possible Jonas would fire him to get him out of her life.

Nick assumed his superiors had considered this risk and were willing that he take it in an effort to move the investigation forward more quickly.

It was early evening when he changed out of his

jeans and T-shirt and into a gray suit and black dress shirt and headed for Jonas's place. He had a tidbit of information he knew would only serve to ingratiate him further into Jonas's confidence.

By this time Jonas should be settled in and they should already have eaten the evening meal. Hopefully it was a perfect time to drop in.

As he drove toward the luxury mansion, he thought again of his new directive. Time to play Post Office. He'd kissed the prettiest girl in the sixth grade in a game of Post Office at a birthday party when he'd been eleven years old.

This game of Post Office wouldn't be as innocent. Nick wasn't particularly thrilled at the prospect of using any woman as a tool, but Lynnette might be the only way to get to her godfather. The stakes were too high, and Jonas White had to be brought down.

Jonas and his goddaughter lived like royalty. The mansion they called home was a self-sustaining compound complete with backup generators, intensive security and luxuries most people only dreamed about.

Although Nick had been in the house on occasion, there were many of the thirty rooms that he'd not been in, rooms that he knew contained the heart of Jonas's illegal operations. Hopefully Lynnette White would be his key into those rooms.

He pulled up before the heavy iron gate and punched in the security code that would allow him entry. When his car went through, the gates closed behind him and he pulled around the circular driveway and stopped before the front door of the house.

He was aware of the fact that his approach had been watched by dozens of guards. As head of security, Nick had hired the men who were responsible for the safety of Jonas and the members of the household.

He also couldn't help but notice another car in the driveway, one he recognized as belonging to Richard Dunst. Nick grimaced with distaste. Dunst had also been on the FBI radar for years. He was another man who needed to be brought down and put behind bars for the rest of his life.

Nick's knock on the front door was answered by Rita Batista, the housekeeper. Her broad face lit with a smile as she ushered him inside the foyer. "Good to see you, Mr. Nick. I'll tell Mr. Jonas that you wish to speak with him," she said. Even though she'd been in the United States for years, her voice still held the heavy accent of her Cuban roots. "He and Mr. Richard and Miss Lynn are in the family room."

She disappeared, leaving Nick to cool his heels in the foyer. Although Nick knew what he had to do where Lynnette was concerned, he also knew that particular directive would take time and finesse and would best be accomplished when Jonas left town once again and Miss Lynn would be more vulnerable.

He smiled as Jonas approached him, a hand stretched out in greeting. "Nick...how are you?"

Nick grabbed his hand in a firm handshake. "I'm fine, sir. And welcome home."

"Thank you. I love traveling, but it's always good to come home and touch base." At sixty-three years old and standing over six feet tall, Jonas was a daunting figure in spite of the fact that his black hair had become more sparse in recent years. His dark eyes held not only a keen intelligence, but also a soulless quality that could chill to the bone.

He was dressed in a pair of tan dress slacks and beige-and-white shirt that probably cost as much as Nick's little cottage.

"I'm sorry to interrupt your homecoming celebration, but I have a bit of information I thought might interest you." Just as Nick suspected, Jonas's dark eyes lit in anticipation.

"Come into the study," he said, and led Nick toward the room that was most familiar. It was in the impressive study that Nick usually met with Jonas for security updates and other business.

Jonas gestured Nick into a chair in front of the ornate mahogany desk, but remained standing himself. He looked at Nick expectantly.

"It's come to my attention through certain contacts that the Marconi family is about to splinter into two warring factions," Nick said. He knew Jonas wouldn't ask about his source of the information, knew that Jonas was aware of Nick's background as the youngest son of a powerful organized-crime family in Miami.

Although Jonas had no specific ties to any organized-crime faction, he liked having an inside source inform him about what was going on and who was in power. Jonas was always looking for a way to exploit or gain strength in the underworld where he functioned.

Jonas's dark eyebrows pulled together in a speculative frown. "Interesting."

"My sources tell me Marconi's right-hand man, Ricky Sanford, is disgruntled and overly ambitious and is about to set up business on his own. I'd say within the next week he'll either be dead or in control."

"And if you were a betting man?"

"I'd bet that he'll take control," Nick said.

Jonas nodded. "I appreciate you bringing this to me, Nick," he said as Nick got up from the chair.

Jonas clapped him on the back as the two of them walked out of the study. "Why don't you go on inside the family room and keep Lynn company for a few minutes while I have a little chat with Richard."

Nick was surprised by the suggestion. Normally Jonas would have thanked him and walked him to the front door. He realized that his information had done just what he'd hoped it would do... move him further into Jonas's confidence.

They walked together to the family room where Lynn sat on one end of a deep burgundy leather sofa and Dunst sat on the other end.

Lynn looked distinctly uncomfortable. It was difficult to discern whether Dunst was uncomfortable or not. Nick had never seen his facial features display any kind of emotion at all.

"Richard...we need to talk," Jonas said and indicated the bald man should follow him back to the study. "Nick, say hello to Lynnette."

"Hello, Lynnette," Nick said and smiled at the beautiful young woman he hoped to seduce and use to bring down the empire of the man who had raised her.

Chapter 2

"Lynn, honey, keep Nick company while Richard and I talk in the study."

Lynn watched in panic as Jonas and Richard left the room. She stood, a ripple of nervous energy making it impossible for her to remain seated. "Good evening, Mr. Barnes," she forced out the words. "Would you care for a drink?"

"Sure, a scotch on the rocks would be great, and, please, make it Nick." He smiled, a lazy, sexy smile, and Lynn felt a curl of heat unfurl in her stomach. He had the nicest voice, deep and smooth.

She moved to the wet bar in the corner of the room,

grateful to have something to do. She'd never spent any real time with Nick, had only seen him on brief occasions over the two years he'd worked for Jonas. But something about him always made her nervous.

Maybe it was because the man was far too good-looking, with his thick, dark hair and brooding, dark eyes. He wore a suit better than any man she'd ever seen and the first time she'd seen him in a pair of jeans and a T-shirt, her heart had stutter-stepped at the vision.

It wasn't just his physical appearance she found appealing. Self-confidence oozed from him, and she had the feeling that he was a man who never suffered shyness or any feeling of inadequacy. Her natural shyness kicked into high gear.

She poured his drink, then walked back to where he still stood, his dark eyes watching her intently. "Please, sit down," she said as she handed him the drink.

"After you." He swept his hand toward the sofa where she'd been sitting before he'd arrived.

She sank down on the buttery-soft leather couch and tried to ignore the flutter in her stomach as he sat next to her, too close for comfort. The familiar shyness built to tormenting proportions as they sat for a moment in uncomfortable silence.

"How's grad school? Jonas says you're doing very well."

A shaft of surprise swept through her. Jonas talked about her to Nick? For the first time she realized Nick's position with her godfather was apparently closer than she had thought. "It's good. I enjoy it."

"Computer science, right?"

"Right." She didn't look at him, but could feel his gaze on her face. The scent of his cologne whispered in the air from his direction, an intensely pleasant scent.

She was vaguely surprised that Jonas had invited Nick to stay, definitely surprised that he'd left her in charge of entertaining him. It was a break from routine that was both unexpected and more than a little bit exhilarating.

"What else do you like to do, Lynnette, besides school?"

She forced herself to turn her head and look at him in an attempt to overcome her shyness.

She couldn't very well tell him she loved breaking into museums and homes and eluding security guards. She certainly couldn't tell him that she loved to run faster than the wind with a prized treasure tucked in her pocket.

"I don't know. I enjoy meeting at the Coffee Cloister with my friends. I like designing video games on the computer. I like going for drives in my car." He had the darkest eyes and the longest eyelashes. She averted her gaze and stared at the pattern of the Oriental rug on the floor.

"Late-night drives," he said softly.

She jerked her head up to look at him once again. Did he know? Had he somehow figured out what she did on those nights she left the house in the dark? As head of security he would know that she occasionally sneaked out of the house when Arturo and Rita were sound asleep.

He smiled at her obvious look of panic. "Don't worry, your secret is safe with me. Is it a guy? Are you dating somebody Jonas wouldn't approve of?"

Her panic subsided as quickly as it had risen. "No, it's nothing like that," she said in relief. She felt the blush that swept over her cheeks. "I just like to take long drives at night. I have insomnia, and a drive in the car always relaxes me. Jonas is so overly protective. If he knew, he'd worry." That wasn't exactly true. Of course Jonas knew she left the house at night to conduct the work that was so important.

"So, no boyfriend?"

"No…there's nobody special."

His gaze swept over her slowly, languidly. "That's surprising. I'd think somebody like you would have dozens of men knocking down your door. No boyfriend." He smiled once again, that sexy smile of his. "I guess that's good news for me."

He had a nice smile, one that involved all his features. The center of his dark eyes sparkled, and the chiseled lines of his face softened with the gesture.

Once again she looked down at the rug as his words caused her heart to beat a strange, new rhythm.

"Ah, good. I see Lynn got you a drink," Jonas said as he returned to the room with Richard Dunst trailing behind him. "Lynn, honey, why don't you make me another one. Richard?"

"Nothing for me."

As the men settled into chairs, Lynn returned to the bar. What she'd like to do was escape to her room and think about how Nick's gaze had caused her to feel momentarily naked...and excited.

She'd like to think about what Nick had meant by his words. *That's good news for me.* The words played and replayed in her mind as she fixed Jonas his usual gin and tonic.

Minutes later they sat and listened as Jonas regaled them with his latest escapades from his travels. Jonas loved an audience, but Lynn had heard most of his stories a hundred times before.

It was easy for her to tune him out and instead focus her attention on Nick. With the simple words he had spoken, he had captured her attention as he never had before. She knew he'd worked for Jonas for a couple of years, knew that Jonas seemed to be depending on Nick more and more, but that was all she knew about him.

There was a part of Lynn that knew she'd be smart to be wary of him. When it came time for somebody

to take over Jonas's defense contracting work and im-
port/export business interests, she didn't intend for
that person to be anyone but herself.

Maybe he'd just been brown-nosing her, sucking up
to the boss's daughter. All her life Jonas had warned
her about people taking advantage of her. He'd in-
grained in her the fact that her position as his goddaughter and her unusual special talents put her at risk.

Still, whether Nick was sucking up to her or not,
she couldn't control the slight shivery warmth he created inside her when he looked at her with those dark
brown eyes of his.

In truth, she was tired of being wary, of not having
a life. She knew Jonas wanted only the best for her,
but lately she'd been chafing at her confines, hungry
for new experiences and to get a taste of real life.

"I'll be flying out again first thing in the morning."

Lynn focused back on the conversation in time to
hear Jonas. "So soon?" she asked in dismay. He'd
only just gotten home. They'd hardly had an opportunity to talk to each other.

"Sorry, honey. You know the state of world affairs.
My work is more important than ever right now."
Jonas finished his drink and set his glass on the mar-
ble-topped table next to his chair.

"Where are you off to?" Nick asked.

"Here and there." Jonas smiled enigmatically. "I'm
afraid I can't be more specific than that."

"Are you traveling with him?" Nick asked of Richard.

"No. I'll be taking care of things here while Jonas is away." Although not a muscle in Richard's face moved, his hazel eyes were cold…reptilian as he stared at Nick.

Richard gave Lynn the creeps. He'd worked for Jonas for as long as Lynn could remember and he'd always given her the creeps. She'd often wondered why he shaved his head, and she thought he wore colored contacts, although she couldn't be sure.

She was grateful when Jonas called an end to the evening and both Nick and Richard departed, leaving her and her godfather alone.

"I wish you didn't have to leave so soon," she said. She loved it when Jonas was in the house. He breathed life into the otherwise silent tomb they called home.

"You know I hate it when I have to leave you, baby." Jonas gazed at her affectionately. "But duty calls and you know how important my work is. Not just to me, but to our country."

"I know. I'm just so lonely when you're away."

Jonas got up from his chair and joined her on the sofa. He placed an arm around her shoulder and pulled her into an embrace. "I know you get lonely, and I wish I could do something to help ease that loneliness. But you also know how dangerous it is for you to get too close to anyone. Casual friends are fine, but anything else is dangerous for you."

Yes, she knew. She'd cut her teeth on the fear that Jonas had instilled in her for as long as she could remember. Closeness bred familiarity, and familiarity bred the sharing of secrets. Jonas had warned her that telling her secrets could get her in trouble. She sighed and felt the familiar restlessness ripple through her.

"We've talked about this many times," Jonas said. "You're special and the very things that make you special also put you at risk to be kidnapped or worse." He tightened his arm around her. "If anything ever happened to you, I'd be lost. You must be careful, Lynn, and you should trust nobody."

"I know...I know."

"I have a little news that might cheer you up." He released her and stood once again. "I've been in touch with our contact, who has been in touch with the Egyptian government concerning a certain artifact that needs to be recovered."

Lynn sat up straighter, a burst of adrenaline flooding through her veins. "What kind of artifact?"

"A solid-gold vase that is believed to have belonged to Queen Hatshepshut. It was unearthed and smuggled out of Egypt by an American archeologist, and Egypt wants it back."

"What are the details?" She sat forward on the sofa.

"I don't have many to give you. The piece is currently on display at the Markham Convention Center.

That's all I know at this time. You'll need to research it while I'm away."

Lynn frowned, remembering the questions that had bothered her the night before when she'd retrieved the diamond. "I don't understand. If the piece is stolen and is being displayed in a public place, why can't the police just go in and arrest the person who has possession of it and give it back to the Egyptian government?"

He finished his drink and stood and faced her. "These things are complicated, Lynn. There are all kinds of political ramifications concerning the work we do. I'm sure you've noticed there is never any publicity about the treasures you've managed to retrieve."

She nodded. "And I've wondered about that, too."

"Lynn, if you aren't comfortable doing this kind of work anymore, you certainly aren't obliged to continue." His voice held a slightly cool disapproval. "I can just let my contact know that we're no longer interested in working for them. I'm sure they have other people as skilled, as competent as you."

"No, it isn't that," she said hurriedly. "It's just that it's all rather confusing to me." She couldn't stand the thought of disappointing Jonas.

"My dear, working for the government is always confusing," Jonas said with a laugh. He sobered. "You have to trust me, Lynn. What we're doing is a service to our country."

"Of course I trust you," she replied. How could she not trust him? He'd acted as her mother and father since she'd been a baby. She adored him with all her heart.

"Then we can depend on you in this matter?"

"Of course you can…always," she replied.

"Good! And now I must say good-night," Jonas said. "I have an early flight in the morning."

She wanted to protest. They'd scarcely had any time together, and he'd be gone in the morning. But she didn't protest. She'd learned long ago to merely accept what little time her godfather had to give her.

"Good night, Uncle Jonas." She stood and kissed him on the cheek. As she watched him disappear up the staircase toward his master suite, she realized he hadn't really answered any of her questions at all.

The next day as she sat with several friends at a table in the Coffee Cloister, an upscale coffee shop near the college campus, the last thing on her mind was the work she did for the government and her godfather.

The conversation between the four young women, as always, revolved around clothes and guys, sex and love. As the three others talked about their problems with their boyfriends and ex-boyfriends, Lynn's thoughts turned to Nick.

There had been something in his eyes last night, an expression that had made her slightly breathless with excitement. He hadn't looked at her as if she was the boss's daughter. He had looked at her as though she was an attractive, desirable woman.

She had access to his personnel files through her godfather's computer. She made a mental note to check him out, see what she could learn about the handsome Nick Barnes.

"Earth to Lynn," Jenny Walbrook said, the impatience in her tone indicating it wasn't the first time she'd spoken to Lynn.

"Sorry, what did you say?"

"I asked if you've been to that new little boutique that just opened over on Palm Drive."

"No. The last thing I need is more clothes. Uncle Jonas brings me something new to wear every time he goes out of town. I've got things hanging in my closet with the tags still on them."

"Honey, a woman can never have too many clothes," Jenny said.

"Or too-thin thighs," Vicki added and they all laughed. The ring of Lynn's cell phone interrupted the laughter. She rummaged in her purse to get it.

"Right on time," Sonya Kincaid said dryly as she looked at her watch. "We've been here fifteen minutes and he's checking up on her."

Lynn ignored her friends as she answered the phone. "Hi, Uncle Jonas," she said, knowing it could only be him. He was the only person who ever called her cell phone.

"Where are you, my dear?" he asked.

"At the Coffee Cloister with some friends," she replied.

"How long are you planning on staying?"

The phone call and the question weren't unusual. Jonas often called to see where she was, whom she was with and how long she'd be gone.

His overprotectiveness had never bothered her much before, but today she found the phone call irritating. She was an adult, yet she had to answer to Jonas as if she were ten years old and spending time away from home for the very first time.

"I'll be home when we finish having coffee." She rolled her eyes for the benefit of her friends and tamped down an unexpected edge of resentment toward her godfather.

"You know I worry when you're out and about," he said.

"I know, but I assure you I'm fine and will be home later." It was the same conversation she had with him over and over again on a daily basis. They said their goodbyes and Lynn hung up and dropped her cell phone back into her purse.

"Honestly, Lynn. I don't know how you stand it," Vicki Taylor said the moment Lynn had hung up. "I mean, we all have people who care about us, but your godfather definitely takes the prize for being the most obsessive."

"I know," Lynn replied. She also knew that within the next fifteen or twenty minutes Jonas would call again to see if she'd made it home yet or not. It was rare that he didn't call three or four times during the time she spent with her friends after classes.

"I don't know how you can have a normal life with him calling you all the time," Vicki continued. "I mean, don't you ever just want to take that cell phone and toss it into the ocean?"

"Only about twice a day," Lynn replied, then breathed a sigh of relief as the conversation moved to other subjects.

Lynn couldn't very well tell her friends that her safety had always been an issue. Not only did Jonas worry about her being kidnapped for ransom because of his incredible wealth, but also because of the special powers she possessed.

She'd often wondered where she'd gotten the special skills that came so naturally...the acute hearing, the unnatural strength and speed, the sharp senses of smell and sight and feel.

Jonas had always told her they were gifts of nature. He'd had a large part in honing those gifts, seeing to it, also, that she had been trained in self-defense and martial arts.

Yes, she loved Jonas dearly and knew he'd done wonderful things for her and worried obsessively about her. But lately she was growing more and more irritated by all of the constraints he placed on her.

She wondered what would happen if she just didn't answer the phone. What would Jonas do if several hours passed and he couldn't get in touch with her? She was surprised to realize the thought held a certain appeal.

"Why don't you meet us tonight, Lynn?" Sonya said as she flipped a strand of her platinum-blond hair behind her ear. "It's Friday night and you never go with us to Sensations."

Sensations was a popular Miami nightclub where Lynn knew her three friends hung out regularly on the weekends. She'd never gone with them. In fact, Lynn had never been inside a nightclub before.

"Oh, I don't know," she began her usual protests.

"Come on, Lynn. What's one night of cutting loose a little bit? All you do is go to classes and study. It's not natural. Come out with us and have some fun tonight," Vicki said.

"Do it, Lynn," Jenny reached across the small table and grabbed Lynn's hand. "We usually meet there around nine and we always have such a good time. It just isn't normal for a twenty-two-year-old to spend every night at home."

Lynn's usual protest rose to her lips, but this time, instead of voicing it, she swallowed hard. Did she dare? Jonas would have a fit if he knew she was even contemplating a night at a club.

"All right, I'll meet you all there around nine this evening." The minute the words left her mouth a thrill of anticipation whirled through her.

Tonight she would go to the club and hang out with her friends. If Jonas called her on the cell phone she wouldn't answer it. She was twenty-two years old. It was time for her to rebel a bit against the lifestyle that had become far too constrictive.

It was time she got a life, a real life. She couldn't wait.

Shy and beautiful, those were the words to describe Lynnette White. Nick sat in his office in the outbuilding that served as security headquarters for the compound and thought about Lynnette and the few minutes they had spent alone together the night before.

She was like a hothouse flower, and why wouldn't she be? For the two years that Nick had worked for Jonas, and from everything he'd learned in that time, she'd certainly been treated like a hothouse flower.

Homeschooled through high school, driven back and forth in a car with a bodyguard through college, she'd definitely not had what could be considered a normal lifestyle.

He checked his watch and jumped up out of his chair. She should be pulling through the gates in the next ten minutes or so and he intended to be waiting for her.

As he left the outbuilding, his gaze automatically swept the grounds. Jonas's illegal activities paid very well. It was Nick's job to see that his security wasn't breached.

Surveillance cameras were hidden throughout the property, keeping electronic vigil to make certain the perimeters of the grounds weren't breached.

Behind the main house was a small shed where Nick and his team did most of their work. There, a huge bank of video screens monitored every area of the property.

There was also a force of security guards that kept an eye on the area immediately around the house. Jonas didn't take his security lightly and neither did Nick.

As he walked, thoughts of Lynnette once again played in his mind. Somehow the fact that she was shy and so protected made his job to seduce her all the more distasteful. If she were worldly, savvy to the ways of people, and men in particular, he wouldn't feel the tinge of regret that played in him now.

Still, it had to be done. He'd worked for two years to get into the inner workings of Jonas's illegal activities and had yet to fully gain the man's trust. His supervisors at the FBI had decided the way in was through Lynnette, so that's the way Nick would go. He had his orders, and Nick tried to always follow orders.

Of course, it had been his penchant for not following orders that had first garnered him attention as a raw recruit years ago. He'd gone from raw recruit to deep undercover in the space of weeks. He knew part of his notorious quick climb through the ranks was not only because of his skill and commitment, but also who and where he'd come from.

He shoved these thoughts aside as he reached the front of the mansion and looked at his watch once again. There was no routine when it came to Lynnette's near-nightly sojourns, but during the day you could set a clock by her comings and goings.

She left the house at seven-thirty in the morning on Mondays, Wednesdays and Fridays for eight-o'clock classes and returned home between three and three-fifteen in the afternoons.

He knew her classes ended at two and she often went to coffee with friends afterward, but she never stayed longer than an hour or so.

He leaned against the garage to wait for her arrival home. The July sun beat down relentlessly but Nick didn't mind the heat. He'd been born and raised in Florida, and heat and humidity were part of the package. He could smell the faint briny scent of the ocean and couldn't imagine living anywhere else.

He straightened as he saw Lynnette's smart little red sports car pull up in front of the heavy iron gates of the compound. She had the convertible top down and her chestnut-colored hair sparkled with blond highlights in the sunshine.

He knew the moment she spied him. As she pulled her car up toward the garage and where he stood, he saw her cheeks flame with scarlet color.

She shut off the engine, and in three long strides he was at her door. "Hi," he said as he opened the car door.

"Hi," she replied. "Thank you," she said as she grabbed her books and laptop computer and got out of the car.

He slammed the door shut behind her, noticing as he had the night before that she was much prettier up close than her pictures depicted.

The photos he'd studied of her hadn't begun to capture the intriguing hue of her eyes, a green-and-gold blend that was distinctly unusual. "How was school today?" he asked.

"Fine." She shifted her books from one arm to the other, not quite meeting his gaze.

"Beautiful day, isn't it?" Who would have thought when he'd joined the FBI that part of his job would be making small talk with a shy, beautiful woman?

"Yes, it is pretty." She met his gaze for the first time since she'd gotten out of her car. There was an unexpected boldness in those eyes. "What are you doing, Nick?"

"What do you mean? I'm standing here talking to you."

Her eyes narrowed slightly. "And why are you

doing that? I mean, you've been working for Jonas for a long time and you've never really talked to me before."

Nick was slightly taken aback. He reminded himself that just because she was shy didn't mean she was stupid...quite the contrary. "I don't know. I enjoyed seeing you, talking to you last night. I realized I'd like to talk to you some more, get to know you better."

"Why?" Dark distrust shone from her beautiful eyes, making them more green than gold.

A small laugh burst from him. "Why? Why not?"

The distrust in her eyes grew more pronounced. "And it doesn't hurt to brown-nose the boss's daughter, right?"

"Is that what you think this is about?"

"Isn't it?" She held his gaze for another long moment. There was an edge to her, an edge that hadn't been there the night before. He didn't know what had caused it, but there was a spark in her eyes that looked mischievous, almost dangerous. It was definitely intriguing.

"No, it isn't," he protested, although she was too close for comfort with her assessment of his intentions. "Lynnette, I don't know whether you've noticed or not, but you're a very pretty woman. You're twenty-two, I'm twenty-nine. I work here and you live here. I'd say it's only natural that I'd take an interest in you."

He held his breath, waiting for a response from her. He hadn't expected her to be so suspicious. He hadn't expected her to have such a low opinion of herself that she would just assume any interest on a male's part would be because of ulterior motives.

She frowned and cocked her head to one side. "Richard's coming."

"Excuse me?"

"Richard Dunst," she replied, and looked toward the gate.

Nick followed her gaze, and a moment later Richard's car came into view. "How'd you know?" He turned to look at her once again.

Her cheeks blushed with color. "I heard his car engine. It has a distinctive sound."

Nick had heard nothing until Richard's car had pulled up to the gate. But he got no opportunity to ask her about it as Richard parked his car behind hers and got out and approached them.

Nick felt himself tense as Dunst drew closer. He sensed Lynnette tensing, as well. As far as the FBI was concerned, Jonas White was the devil himself. But the devil had a right-hand man and that was Richard Dunst.

"Nick…Lynn." Richard greeted them with a curt nod of his closely shaved head. "I need to get some papers from inside for Jonas."

Rumor had it the man had at some point in the past

gone under the knife of a bad plastic surgeon. Something had gone wrong and that's why Richard's face appeared masklike, incapable of displaying any real emotion.

Nick could tell the man wore contacts, but nothing could hide the cold evil that resided within. Nick hoped that when they brought down Jonas, Richard fell with him. Nothing would give Nick more pleasure than to slap a tight pair of handcuffs on the man. Maybe then his features would express some emotion.

Dunst's gaze went from Lynnette back to Nick. "Is there a security problem?"

"No, nothing like that. I was just visiting with Lynnette." As if it were any of Dunst's business, Nick thought.

"And I was just on my way inside," Lynnette said. She moved past Nick and toward the front door, Richard just behind her.

When she reached the door, she opened it to allow Richard to precede her, then she turned back to Nick. A tiny smile curved up the corners of her full lips.

"My friends call me Lynn and tonight around nine I'm going to be at Sensations, a dance club in Miami." With these words and a sweet blush, she turned and disappeared into the house.

He reared back on his heels and shoved his hands

in his pockets as he took in her words. It had sounded like an invitation to join her.

Maybe seducing Lynn wasn't going to be quite as difficult as he'd initially thought.

Chapter 3

It was about a thirty-minute drive from Jonas's house to the outskirts of Miami where the club Sensations was located. As Lynn zipped down the highway toward the club, her heart beat rapidly with excitement.

She'd spoken with Jonas only an hour before and didn't expect him to call the rest of the night. When she'd spoken to him, she'd told him she was lying on her bed studying, which had been true at the time. She just didn't mention that she intended to get up and go out.

She didn't want to lie to him, but she knew he'd disapprove of her plans for the night. He'd fill her head with stories of danger and kidnapping and he'd wear her down until she agreed to stay home.

She was tired of staying home, tired of being followed around the house by little blinking red lights and having only Arturo and Rita for company. She was tired of living like Rapunzel in her tower, protected from life by fear and an overly protective godfather.

Most evenings she spent on her computer, messing around with the video game she was programming or chatting in chat rooms. Although she'd always enjoyed the interaction with other people, she was also always aware that the relationships she had with her cyber friends were superficial and not real.

Again a wave of adrenaline shot through her. Tonight she was going to enjoy life the way most women her age enjoyed it…without fear, without restraints.

She was going to have a couple of drinks with her friends, dance to the music and act like a normal, healthy young woman. Tonight she was going to interact with real people in a real environment instead of in cyberspace with user names.

She'd never done anything like this before. She'd never rebelled in any way against Jonas and his fears and worries over her safety. She adored Jonas, who had taken her in after her parents' deaths when she'd been five months old, saving her from a life as a ward of the state.

Her single goal through childhood and adolescence had been to please Jonas. She'd spent all of her life seeking his approval by being the good, dutiful daughter. She'd wanted to show him that he hadn't made a mistake when he'd adopted her and brought her into his home to raise.

Certainly he'd given her the best of everything, and she never doubted that he had her best interests at heart. But the restlessness that she'd felt for the past several months could no longer be silenced.

It was time for her to seek her own way, find out who she was separate from Jonas. It was definitely time for a change.

Although she had never been to the dance club, she'd driven by it once not too long ago when she'd come into Miami to pick up some school supplies.

The closer she got, the faster her heart beat with excitement. She felt as if this was the first night of her life, that finally she was going to break free from who and what she was and just have fun like any normal twenty-two-year-old.

The club was housed in a huge steel-and-glass one-story building with bright neon lettering flashing across the top. The parking lot was already three-quarters filled when Lynn turned in at ten after nine.

She spied Sonya's silver Porsche and pulled into the empty space next to it. She sat for a moment in the car, fighting the shyness that always swept over her when she was going into unknown territory. Go have some fun, she commanded herself.

As she stepped out of her car, the balmy night air wrapped around her, bringing with it the scent of the city and the sounds of music and people, coming from the open door of the club.

A touch of nerves fluttered in her stomach as she reached up and smoothed her hair, then ran her clammy hands down the thighs of her tight jeans.

Her blouse was a forest-green crop top that she knew enhanced the green of her eyes. The blouse displayed her slender waist and was more provocative than her usual choice. She figured if she was going to cut loose, she might as well dress the part.

She grabbed her tiny purse from the car seat, then locked the car and walked toward the front door of the club. Her friends had been talking about Sensations forever. She knew from them that the place had become one of the hot spots of Miami for the young and single set.

A man at the door collected the ten-dollar cover charge, then Lynn walked past him and into the nightclub. For just a moment she was overwhelmed with sights and sounds.

The club was cavernous. At the far end a live band played from an elevated stage area. Writhing, gyrating bodies filled the huge dance floor, and colored lights swept over them like beacons drawn to their movements.

Tables were arranged around the dance floor and a long bar stretched across each side of the room. There were people everywhere and Lynn despaired of ever finding her friends in the mesh of people.

"Hey, sweetheart, I haven't seen you around here before. How about you let me buy you a drink?" A tall blonde touched Lynn's arm, his bleary smile letting her know he'd been here awhile and had imbibed more than one drink.

"No, thanks, I'm looking for somebody."

"I'm the man you're looking for," he replied. He paused to sip from the drink glass in his hand, then continued. "I'm the Romeo to your Juliet, the moon to your stars, the music to your song." He smiled with the overconfidence of a drunk, displaying a row of perfect white teeth.

"I'm sorry, but I'm not interested." Lynn felt the blush that heated her cheeks. She wasn't looking for a love connection or a one-night stand. She just wanted a night out with her friends.

At that moment, to her relief, she heard Sonya calling her name. She looked around and spied her friends at a table in the distance. "Excuse me," she said to the blonde. "Maybe another time." She didn't give him an opportunity to say anything else but hurried toward the table where Sonya, Vicki and Jenny were waving to her.

"We thought you were going to chicken out and not

show," Vicki said as she pulled a chair out and yanked Lynn into it.

"I got hung up at the door by some guy who wanted to be the Romeo to my Juliet," Lynn replied.

The three others looked at each other and laughed. "That's Roger," Sonya said. "He's been looking for his Juliet for as long as we've been coming here."

"Drinks! We need drinks," Vicki said, and signaled to a passing waitress.

Within minutes they all had drinks before them. The others had ordered Lynn a drink called an Alabama Slammer, a fruit-punch-like concoction that went down smooth and easy and sweet.

"So, did you sneak out of the house, or tell your uncle you were going to the library to study?" Sonya asked.

"Neither," Lynn replied. "Uncle Jonas is out of the country. I spoke to him on the phone before I left to come here."

"I'll bet a hundred bucks you didn't mention what was on your agenda for the night," Jenny said, her brown eyes sparkling.

Lynn laughed. "No way. I'd lose the bet."

Vicki leaned over and grabbed her arm. "We're just glad you're here. It's about time you get a life."

"I'll drink to that," Lynn replied, and hoisted her glass for a group toast.

Lynn had met the other three women two years

ago when she'd been attending college. They were the only friends she'd ever had, and she adored each of them.

Sonya Kincaid, with her bleached blond hair and love of makeup was a theater major and the extrovert of the three. Currently she worked teaching high school drama and was active in community theater.

Jenny Walbrook was majoring in child psychology and was a slightly overweight brunette with a smile that could warm Antarctica.

Lynn was closest to Vicki Taylor. She'd known the pretty redhead longer than the other two. Vicki was also a computer science grad student. Vicki came from a wonderfully normal, tight-knit middle-class family. Lynn loved hearing her talk about her parents and siblings.

Lynn had never been much of a drinker. She occasionally had a glass of wine with dinner, but the Alabama Slammers were delicious, and the ambiance around her encouraged her to have more than one.

By the time she was halfway through her third drink, she was having a ball. She felt a pleasant buzz in her head and found everything anyone said vastly amusing.

The first time a guy came up and asked her to dance, she'd declined with a fierce blush. She'd never danced in public before, and her natural shyness raised its ugly head.

But, it didn't take her long to realize that nobody was paying attention to anyone else, and the music called to her at the same time the drinks gave her courage. When she was asked again, with her friends urging her on, she hit the dance floor.

She danced and laughed and drank with her old friends and the new friends she met. The loud music made any meaningful conversation impossible, but Lynn didn't mind. With each drink her head grew fuzzier and fuzzier and the last thing she wanted was conversation. She just wanted the music and the laughter and the feeling of utter freedom that sang in her veins.

By the time she finished her fifth drink she was vaguely aware that the fuzz in her brain had grown bigger than anything else.

She grabbed her purse and stumbled toward the rest rooms, deciding that perhaps a cool compress on her forehead would sober her up just a bit.

She was surprised by the way the floor seemed to undulate beneath her feet as she walked slowly and carefully to keep from falling down. Her stomach felt just a tad bit sick, and she stepped up her pace, eager to get to the bathroom.

The rest room was crowded, but she managed to work her way to one of the sinks. She grabbed a couple of paper towels, ran them under the cold water, then wiped them across her forehead and the back of her neck.

Her reflection in the mirror was blurry and she felt as if she were swimming through layers of cotton. The cool water on her neck and forehead did little to clear her head.

So, this is what it felt like to drink too much, she thought. More than anything she suddenly wanted to curl up in a corner and sleep until the brain fogginess passed.

The idea of being found in the morning curled up on the floor by a cleaning crew made her giggle. She swiped her forehead one last time then turned away from the mirror.

As she shuffled from the rest room she vaguely realized she'd learned a valuable lesson tonight…three Alabama Slammers was her absolute limit and at the moment she was way over her limit. If she ever came here again she would know to limit her drinks to no more than three.

She'd gone only a few feet toward the table where her friends awaited when a big hand grabbed her around her upper arm.

"Hey, baby, I think maybe it's time you and I spend a little alone time together."

She squinted up at the tall, dark-haired man who held her in his grip. She'd danced with him twice and thought she might have flirted with him a bit. She thought his name was Bob. "I don't think so, Bob," she said, and attempted to pull her arm from his grasp. "I need to get back to the table with my friends."

"Come on, honey. You know you're hot for me." He pulled her down the hallway back toward the rest rooms, then backed her up and she found herself pinned between him and a wall. "And the name is Rob."

"Bob…Rob…whatever, my friends are waiting for me and I'm not hot for anyone. In fact, I'm not feeling very well." She placed her palms on his massive chest and pushed in an attempt to get some breathing room.

She was uncomfortable by his intimate nearness, and the fact that they appeared to be in a small alcove just out of view of the general public made her even more uneasy.

"I'll make you feel better. Come on, admit it. You've been coming on to me all night long. You've been sending me signals and, honey, I've been receiving them." His breath was hot and sour as he leaned forward, apparently preparing to kiss her.

She turned her head to the side and felt his mouth glance off her cheek. Confusion swept through her. Had she been sending signals? She didn't think so. She certainly hadn't meant to.

"I'm sorry…I didn't mean anything…just let me go," she said, and pushed against his chest again. He was as immovable as a mountain, and the first stir of panic rose up inside her. "Please, let me go."

"I'll let you go when I'm finished getting to know

you better." His blue eyes were cold, hard-looking as he sneered down at her.

To her horror, his hands moved up her body and across her breasts. She wanted to throw up. He pressed more intimately against her, and she could feel that he was aroused.

"I'm warning you, let me go or you'll be sorry."

He laughed, as if stimulated by her protests and pleas. "I'll be sorry? What are you going to do, sweetheart? Hit me with that little purse you're carrying?"

Lynn had never used the skills she'd been born with, outside of her work. Jonas had warned her from the time she was small that those skills should never be used when somebody else could see. But she wasn't about to allow this half-drunk creep to touch her anymore. She drew a deep, steadying breath, then struck out.

He'd been late. A problem with one of the security cameras had caused Nick to be late arriving at Sensations. The moment he'd arrived it had taken him only a few minutes to spy Lynn at the table with her friends.

He'd stood some distance away and watched her. It was obvious she was having a good time. He'd never seen her look so animated, and it was apparent she was comfortable with her friends.

It was also obvious that she'd had a lot to drink when she stood and staggered off toward the rest rooms. He watched her as she made her way across the floor. Her jeans fit tightly on her long, slender legs and sexy bottom. The short blouse displayed her flat abdomen and the thrust of her breasts. She looked hot, and Nick had a feeling he wasn't the only male in the place who had noticed that fact.

When several minutes passed and she didn't come back to her table, Nick headed in the direction of the rest rooms, wondering what was taking her so long.

He saw her immediately, pinned against a wall by a big hulk of a drunk. She looked tiny and helpless and frightened and adrenaline pumped through Nick as he forced his way through the throng of people to get to her.

Before he could reach her, she flew into motion with a speed that astounded Nick. She boxed the man's ears, jabbed him in the eyes, then shoved him back with a force that looked almost inhuman.

"Lynn," he cried to be heard above the noise.

Her eyes were wild as she looked around. When she saw him, she ran into his arms. Nick put an arm around her while he looked for the creep who'd had her backed against the wall. He was nowhere to be seen.

"Are you all right?" he asked her as he put his hands on her slender shoulders.

She nodded and looked up at him, her green eyes overly bright and unfocused. "I'm just so glad to see a familiar face." Her words slurred together so it sounded as if she said "sogladseefamiliarfash." She leaned into him, and he wrapped his arms around her.

"You're drunk," he said.

She nodded, not even bothering to protest his announcement. "Too many 'Bama Slammers."

She didn't seem to notice that she was in his arms. She leaned heavily against him as if unsure she could stand on her own. She might not be aware of their closeness, but he was acutely aware of it.

The top of her head fit neatly just beneath his chin and the soft silk of her chestnut hair tickled his jaw. Her breasts pressed against his chest, and her breath was warm and punch scented on his face.

His hand pressed against her back and encountered the warm skin between her short top and the waistband of her jeans. The touch of her warm, smooth skin electrified him.

"You need to go home," he said gruffly, and moved his arm from around her back.

"You're absolutely right. I'll just say goodbye to my friends and be off." She swayed on her feet without him as an anchor.

Nick cursed under his breath and put his arm around her once again. She was totally bombed. "I'll drive you home," he said.

"That's not necessary," she protested, the words running together to form one long word. "I'm perfectly capable of driving home."

Ah, the confidence of drunks, he thought ruefully. "I'm driving you home, and that's the end of the matter," he said forcefully. "Now, go say goodbye to your friends and we'll get out of here."

As they wove their way back to the table where Lynn's friends sat, Nick kept a firm grip on her, not trusting that she wouldn't fall flat on her face if he let her go.

What would she have done if he hadn't shown up here when he did? Who would have seen to it that she got home safely? He wanted to lecture her on her irresponsibility, drinking too much and not only getting herself in a tight spot with a man, but also not thinking about how she would get herself home safe and sound.

But he knew a lecture at this moment would be wasted on her. Drunks didn't listen to lectures.

"Wow, did you find him in the bathroom?" a heavily made-up blonde at the table asked Lynn with a pale arched eyebrow. "I need to go to the bathroom more often if that's what's available."

Lynn giggled and placed a slender hand on Nick's chest. "These are my friends, Sonya, Vicki and Jenny." She patted his chest. "And this is Nicky. He's driving me home."

The flirtatious smile on Sonya's face instantly disappeared. "Whoa, Lynn, honey. One of us will drive you home. One of the cardinal rules of club life is that you don't let a man you just met take you home when you're drunk."

"I'm not drunk and Nicky is an old friend. He works for Uncle Jonas. I'll be perfectly fine with him."

Nick was impressed that her friends apparently did care enough about her to question his motives. "I'm head of security for Jonas. I'll see that she gets home safely," he said even as he marveled over the fact that she'd called him Nicky and patted him on the chest.

It was obvious her intake of alcohol had quieted the natural shyness he knew she possessed. "Say good-bye, Lynn, and let's get you home."

"Yes, get me home to my ivory tower with the little red eyes that watch me and the cell phone that Uncle Jonas uses to keep track of me twenty-four/seven."

The long sentence seemed to take everything out of her. She slumped against Nick and moaned. "I think I feel sick."

That was Nick's cue to half carry, half drag her to the nearest exit. He hoped when she got some fresh air maybe she'd sober up a bit.

His hope was short-lived. The night air did nothing to sober her up, if anything she appeared to be getting drunker by the moment.

He guided her to his car but paused before putting her in the passenger seat. "Do you feel like you're going to throw up?" He hated to be indelicate, but he didn't want her tossing her cookies in his car.

"No, I don't think so. I just need to close my eyes for a few minutes. Everything is spinning."

He tucked her into the passenger seat, then hurried to the driver's side and slid in behind the wheel. She slumped back, eyes closed and appeared to pass into oblivion as he started the car and left Sensations behind.

As he drove, her scent eddied in the air, the fragrance of expensive spicy perfume and the faint sweet scent of punch and Southern Comfort.

She'd felt good against him. Too good. It had been more than two years since Nick had enjoyed any kind of relationship with a woman. Being undercover wasn't conducive to relationships and usually only led to disaster. He hoped developing a relationship with Lynn wouldn't prove disastrous for either one of them.

He thought of what she'd said when he'd told her it was time to go home, home to her ivory tower where the red eyes followed her and her cell phone rang all the time.

It wasn't much of a life. He knew the red eyes she'd spoken of were the sensors in the walls. Jonas had been enthralled by the technology that would allowed him to see on a computer screen where in the house each member of the household was, to control the temperature of the air, the artwork on the wall, the music that was piped into each individual room.

Jonas had loved the unique technology, but Nick

had never thought about what it would be like to live everyday life with that kind of Big Brother surveillance. Maybe that was another reason for her nightly drives—to escape the ivory tower that was home for a little while.

He had a feeling tonight had been some sort of latent teenage rebellion for Lynn, a bucking and kicking of the rigid rules and isolated lifestyle she lived to please Jonas.

"Nicky?"

He looked over to see her still slumped down, but her beautiful eyes were open and she looked at him. "Yeah?"

"I'm drunk."

He smiled. "Yes, you are."

"I've never been drunk before. I'm not sure I like it."

She sat up and rolled down her window, appearing to sober up just a tad.

"How many drinks did you have?"

She frowned, a delicate furrow appearing between her brows. "I'm not sure…five or six. I think I might have lost count." She tilted her head toward the window, letting the night breeze blow her hair and caress her face.

For a few minutes they rode in silence, then she turned to look at him once again. "Have you ever gotten totally blitzed?"

He laughed. "I'm ashamed to admit, on more than one occasion, although most of my drunks occurred in the six months after my twenty-first birthday."

"Did you feel awful afterward?"

"Each and every time," he admitted.

Once again she fell silent and her eyes drifted closed. He wondered if she'd fallen asleep. If so, it was probably the best thing for her as long as he could rouse her enough to get her into the house when they arrived.

The minute he pulled into the drive and pressed the button on his remote that would open the gates, she sat up and opened her eyes once again.

He parked in front of the door, got out of the car and went around to open her car door. He held out his hand to help her up out of the car. "Are you okay to get inside?"

"I'm fine." She held on to his hand and leaned into him, the warmth of her body stirring an immediate response in his. "You won't tell Uncle Jonas about tonight, will you? He'd be upset with me."

He squeezed her hand. "Don't worry, this will be our little secret."

She smiled, a half-drunk grin that was more than a little bit charming. Her face was mere inches from his. To his surprise she threw her arms around his neck. "Thank you. Maybe we should kiss to seal our secret."

Apparently she hadn't sobered up much at all because Nick knew if she wasn't drunk as a skunk she'd never be acting so forward.

That didn't mean he wasn't tempted. He was definitely tempted. Her lips looked soft and welcoming, but he knew if he took advantage of her now in her condition, he could kiss any hope of a future relationship goodbye.

He skimmed a strand of her silky, chestnut hair from her face and smiled down at her. "When I kiss you, Lynnette White, I want you sober as a preacher and aware of every second of that kiss."

Her eyes widened as he released his hold on her. "If you'd like, I'll be more than happy to drive you back to the club for your car in the morning."

"Okay." She blinked a couple of times, as if the gesture might help her clear her thoughts. "First thing in the morning? Maybe around eight?"

"Why don't we make it around ten," he countered, knowing she had no idea what was in store for her when she woke up in the morning.

"Okay, and thanks again."

"No problem."

She definitely wasn't sober, he thought as he watched her weave her way toward the front door. One thing was clear—tonight certainly hadn't hurt him in his bid to get closer to her.

It wasn't until he was halfway to his own apartment

that he thought of how she'd handled the creep who'd had her pinned against the wall.

He'd never seen anyone move so fast or with such skill. He'd intended to ride in on his white horse and save the day, but she hadn't needed him to help her at all.

He had a feeling there was a lot more to Lynnette White than he'd initially thought. He was aware of the fact that he was probably on a path to destruction no matter how things went.

If he seduced Lynn and learned what he needed to bring Jonas down, then Lynn would live with the consequences of his actions.

If he seduced her and things went bad between them before he got the information he needed, then Jonas would either fire him or kill him.

Nick knew the man was capable of both.

Chapter 4

"Eat your breakfast. Eggs aren't good when they're cold." Rita's dark eyes gazed at Lynn suspiciously. "Are you coming down with something? It isn't like you to dawdle over your food."

Lynn stared down at the eggs on her plate and grimaced. The sunny-side-up eggs appeared to be staring back at her. "No, I'm not coming down with anything. I'm just not very hungry this morning."

She wasn't sick. It was much worse than that. She suspected she was on the verge of death.

She'd awakened forty-five minutes ago feeling as if a hundred drums thundered in her head. She'd still been wearing her clothes from the night before. Her mouth had felt as if it had been stuffed with foul-tasting cotton, and she was certain if she moved too fast she would be dead before she made it out of her bed.

A long, hot shower had done little to still the thunder in her head. She still felt more than a little queasy. She barely remembered falling into bed the night before and had only vague memories of the ride home in Nick's car.

"Are you sure you aren't getting sick?" Rita asked with a frown of concern. "You look pale."

A burst of affection for the frowning Cuban woman filled Lynn. Rita was the closest thing to a mother Lynn would ever know. "Really, I'm fine." To assure the older woman she picked up a piece of toast and bit into it. She thought she could handle toast and coffee.

Rita refilled her own coffee cup and joined Lynn at the kitchen table. "I know what's wrong. You're just missing Mr. Jonas," she exclaimed.

Lynn nodded, relieved to have the subject changed. "It's always difficult for the first couple of days when he leaves after being here. When he's home he fills the house with such energy."

"He spoils you." Rita's dark eyes twinkled. "If you were a different kind of person you would be intolerable from all his spoiling."

Lynn laughed, then sobered. "I would gladly give

up all the things Jonas brings me when he comes home if he would just spend more time here with us."

"He's an important man and does important work. Besides, it won't be long until he'll be home again."

"I know." As Lynn ate her toast Rita talked about her children. She and Arturo had three boys, all older than Lynn and all married with their own families. As always, when Rita spoke of her family, a wistful yearning filled Lynn.

Rita's boys had always been kind to Lynn, but even though Rita and Arturo had been good and loving to her, it wasn't the same as having her own real family.

"Raoul is coming to visit on Sunday," Rita said. "You enjoy visiting with him."

At twenty-five, Raoul was Rita's youngest son and the one closest in age to Lynn. "Yes, it will be nice seeing him again. Is he bringing his wife and kids?" Raoul had a two-year-old and a three-year-old, both boys, and utterly delightful children.

"Not this visit. It will just be Raoul."

Lynn took another bite of her toast and thought about the parents she'd never known. "You didn't know my parents, did you, Rita?" she asked.

Rita shook her head. "No. They were already gone when Mr. Jonas hired us. I only know what you know, that they were close friends to Mr. Jonas and when you were born they named him your godfather."

"Jonas told me they were quite wealthy and eccentric."

"They would have had to have been plain loco to take their yacht out on a day when there were storm warnings."

Rita was right. According to what Jonas had told her, and the copies of news reports he'd saved for her, her parents had taken their yacht out and had been hit by a squall and lost at sea. Jonas, as her godfather, had petitioned the court for and won custody of five-month-old Lynn.

Rita sat at the table until Lynn had finished her toast and coffee then, Lynn headed upstairs to get ready for Nick to pick her up and take her to her car.

Nick. She was embarrassed to see him this morning. She didn't remember everything that had occurred the night before, but she had a definite memory of being in his arms and of being half dragged, half carried to his car.

She remembered his eyes glittering dangerously dark as he'd grabbed her to him after she'd fought off the masher. She also remembered the feel of his tautly muscled chest when she'd patted it. She couldn't believe she'd actually patted him on his chest.

She'd never drink again. She would never get so stupid again. As far as she was concerned her first foray into trying to have a life of her own had been a dismal failure. She'd acted like a fool.

At quarter to ten she walked out the front door to watch for Nick. She was dreading seeing him again, ashamed of her actions the night before and the fact that he'd had to rescue her from her own ignorance.

At least the two aspirins she'd swallowed right after breakfast had taken the edge off the headache that was a reminder of the night activities.

She should have just told Nick she'd take a cab this morning to get her car. Then she wouldn't have had to face him. But even as she thought about it, she knew sooner or later she'd have to see him again. It might as well be first thing this morning.

She tensed as she heard the approach of a familiar car. Not Nick's but rather Richard Dunst's. Lynn had no idea what tied her godfather to the humorless, strange man. Richard had been around for as long as Lynn could remember, but she'd never been comfortable around him.

A moment later his car pulled up in front of her and Richard got out. "Good morning, Lynn," he said. "On your way out?" His shaved head gleamed in the morning sunlight.

She resented the question. She had a feeling that when Jonas was away Richard took it upon himself to keep tabs on her movements. She couldn't very well lie and tell him she wasn't going out. Besides, at that moment Nick's car entered through the gates.

"I'm taking a ride with Nick this morning," she

said. She didn't intend to explain further. It was none of his business. She certainly didn't want him to know that Nick was taking her to her car because she'd gone to a club the night before and had gotten too drunk to drive herself home.

"Indeed?" The single word held no inflection, nor did his face show any expression. "Enjoy yourself." He nodded curtly, then went inside the front door.

She didn't give Nick a chance to get out of the car but opened the passenger door herself and slid inside.

"Good morning," he said. "Everything all right?"

"Yes, I've just never been comfortable around Richard." She instantly bit her tongue. "Sorry, I shouldn't have said that."

"Why? You're not allowed to have negative feelings? Personally, I find him rather creepy."

She cast him a grateful smile.

"At least you look a bit better this morning than you did last night." He put the car into gear and took off. "How's your head?"

"When I first woke up I thought it might explode. I took some aspirin and it's feeling a bit better now." She bit her bottom lip, then continued. "I guess I owe you a big apology."

"For what?" He gave her a sideways glance.

"For being drunk and stupid last night." Her cheeks warmed with a blush.

"No need to apologize. Everyone in the place enjoyed it when you stripped down naked and danced onstage with the band."

She stared at him in horror, then saw the teasing grin and the light of laughter in his eyes. "Stop it," she exclaimed. "I did no such thing." She laughed, her laughter quickly dying. "But, what I did was foolish and immature," she admitted.

"You want a lecture about the dangers of young women getting drunk in bars?"

"No, thanks. Trust me Nick, you couldn't say anything to me that I haven't been telling myself all morning."

"Ah, how quickly things change."

"What do you mean?"

"Last night I was Nicky and today I'm back to being just plain Nick."

The heat in her cheeks intensified and her mind filled with a sudden memory of her not only calling him Nicky, but also patting his chest and asking him to kiss her. "Oh my God," she breathed aloud.

"What?"

"I am so mortified. I just remembered asking you for a kiss last night."

"Consider yourself lucky, a lot of women who drink too much in a bar don't remember anything about the night before."

"I'm sure you're right." She turned her head to look out the passenger window, trying to still the beating of her heart. She remembered more than asking him for a kiss. She now remembered his response to her, that when he kissed her he wanted her stone sober so she'd remember every minute of the kiss.

There was no getting around it. Nick Barnes affected her on a level she'd never felt before. There was a light in his eyes when he looked at her that excited her. The very scent of him stirred her, and that sexy smile of his created a heat in the pit of her stomach she'd never felt before.

He was dressed to kill this morning, wearing a pair of charcoal slacks and a black short-sleeved dress shirt that displayed his biceps. He looked cool and elegant and sinfully handsome.

"Personally, I have one regret about last night," he said.

"What's that?"

His dark eyes swept over her before turning back to focus out the front window. "There you were, looking all hot and sexy in those tight little jeans and blouse and I didn't even get a chance to dance with you."

Hot and sexy. Was that the way he saw her? "Do you like to dance?" she asked, grateful that her voice was steady and didn't betray anything of her inner emotions.

"I like to slow dance. I think it's one of the lost arts of our peers, who seem to prefer jumping around on the dance floor rather than being in each other's arms."

Again those dark eyes of his swept over her. "I'd like to take you dancing sometime."

"I think I'd like that." Her breath caught in the center of her chest. Once again she looked out the window as she imagined being held tightly in his arms as they swayed to soft, romantic music.

"Where did you learn how to fight?"

She turned her head to look at him once again, surprised at the abrupt change of subject. "What do you mean?"

"Last night when I got to the club you were pushed up against a wall by some creep. I tried to get to you to help you out, but before I got there you took care of the problem yourself." His gaze held curiosity. "I've never seen anyone move so fast."

She inwardly cursed her stupidity yet again. Jonas had warned her from the time she was little never to display any show of her skills. In the blink of a few drinks she'd forgotten all she'd been taught.

"I've been trained in self-defense. Uncle Jonas made sure of it," she explained. "He's always been afraid that I'd be kidnapped because of his wealth and the work he does for the government with defense contracts and such."

He cast her a look that appeared to be full of surprise, then returned his gaze out the window. "He does seem to have his finger in a lot of pies," he said as he changed lanes and they flew down the highway.

"Yes, he does. I know that besides the import business and his contract work he dabbles in real estate, among other things." She felt herself relaxing with each mile that passed. "What about your family? Do you have relatives here in town?"

She saw his fingers tighten around the steering wheel. "My mother and father live here in Miami, and I've got two brothers and a sister, but I haven't seen any of them for years."

She looked at him in surprise. As someone who'd always hungered for a real family of her own, she couldn't imagine such a thing...to have a big family in the same city and not see them every day. "Why don't you see them?"

He hesitated a long moment before replying. "You ever heard of Joey Barnes?"

Lynn frowned thoughtfully. "Isn't he some sort of Mafia guy?"

"Not Mafia, but organized crime. He's the head of a large crime network here in Miami and he's my father."

Lynn gasped in shock as she digested this information about him. She'd have never guessed. "Does Jonas know about this?"

"Yes, he's aware of my background."

"You don't see your family at all?"

His fingers seemed to relax their hold on the steering wheel. "When I was eighteen I realized I didn't want to be part of my father's lifestyle. I wanted to make my own way in the world. When I told my father that, he disowned me. I occasionally talk to my older brother, Anthony, and my mother, but that's it."

"When you were eighteen, is that when you started your security business?"

"No, I didn't start that until about seven years ago. Between the ages of eighteen and twenty-one, I just kind of drifted, trying to decide exactly what I wanted to do with my life."

"Still, it must be hard not to have any real contact with your family." She sighed wistfully. "I'd give anything to be able to talk to my mother and father or to have sisters and brothers in my life," she said.

"What did happen to your parents? I know Jonas raised you from the time you were a baby."

"Their boat capsized in a storm and they were lost. I was too young to even have any memories of them." She leaned her head back against the seat and smiled. "When I was younger, I went through a period when I was certain that someplace out in the world I had siblings."

"Do you think that's possible?" Nick asked.

"No. It was illogical for me to even entertain the notion, but I guess it was kind of like kids who dream up imaginary friends."

"You must have had a lonely childhood."

She hesitated a moment, then nodded. "Jonas has

been loving and very good to me but he's gone so much of the time. Rita and Arturo have also been as close to family as can be, but, yes, I guess I did have a lonely childhood. Jonas has always been so protective."

Nick glanced at her, then returned his attention back to the road. "I'd say that's the understatement of the century. You mentioned last night something about being in a tower with blinking red eyes and cell phones that never stop ringing."

Lynn gasped and covered her mouth in horror. "I left my cell phone at home."

"Do you need to make a phone call?"

"No, but Jonas will probably be trying to call me." She couldn't believe she'd gone off without the phone. Apparently the fog in her brain from last night hadn't completely disappeared.

"So, he won't be able to reach you until you get back home. What's the problem?"

Indeed? What was the problem? She leaned her head back against the seat thoughtfully. Was it such a crime if Jonas didn't know her every movement, her exact whereabouts at all times of the day or night?

What other person her age had a parent figure checking up on them every couple of hours each day? She had to gain some independence in order to grow. Suddenly she didn't care that Jonas couldn't get ahold of her.

All too quickly they were back at the club. The only car in the lot was hers. "So, what's on your agenda for the rest of the day?" he asked as he parked next to her car.

"Nothing particular," she replied. "What about you?"

"I'm on security duty at noon today."

"Then I've taken up too much of your time already." She opened the passenger door and grabbed her purse from the seat between them. "Thanks again, Nick."

"No problem, and Lynn...if you remember asking me for a kiss last night, do you also remember what my response was?"

His eyes were dark and provocative as he held her gaze.

"That you'd kiss me when I was sober and could remember everything about the kiss." She repeated the words he'd said to her the night before.

He nodded, that sexy grin sweeping over his lips. "You just let me know when you're ready, and I'll be more than happy to oblige you."

"I'll keep that in mind," she said.

Minutes later as she drove back toward home, her thoughts were filled with Nick Barnes. She tried to tell herself that he was probably just being kind, being sociable to the boss's daughter, but she knew it was more than that.

He didn't look at her as the boss's daughter. He looked at her as an attractive, desirable woman. Besides, surely he knew that sucking up to her would get him nowhere with Uncle Jonas.

Lynn recognized she was fairly naive in the arena of dating. Although she'd dated several men over the last couple of years, most of those dates had been arranged by Jonas for social events they were attending all together.

She'd met a few guys at college but nobody who affected her like Nick did. Her attraction to him was visceral, but that wasn't all there was to it.

For some reason she found him easy to talk to, didn't feel the suffocating shyness with him, and that merely increased her attraction to him.

He'd said he'd like to take her dancing sometime, and she was disappointed that he hadn't made any real date with her.

She shoved thoughts of him out of her mind and instead thought of the new job Jonas had pointed out to her, the recovery of the solid-gold vase that was on display at the Markham Center.

She'd spent much of the day yesterday on the Internet studying the floor plans of the building and reading up on anything she could find concerning the Markham Convention Center. There wasn't a computer file in the world she couldn't access, and she'd pulled up everything she could find on the convention center.

From studying the material she knew how to get in and out of the building and knew exactly what she had to do to retrieve the vase once inside. She'd done her homework and planned to execute the recovery that night.

The weather report predicted clouds moving in, and a cloudy night was perfect for her to do her work. Maybe by focusing on the work she loved, she'd stop thinking about Nick Barnes.

Jonas White stood at the window in his hotel room in Paris, the telephone pressed to his ear. He listened as Richard Dunst updated him on some of their business dealings. They were careful about what they said, knowing that Jonas was under FBI investigation and land phone lines could be tapped.

"I smell a romance brewing," Dunst said, when they'd finished their business talk.

"A romance? What are you talking about?"

"Lynn. She apparently has a new suitor. I saw her leaving this morning to take a drive with him."

Jonas tightened his grip on the receiver. So, this was probably why she hadn't answered his calls that morning. A sick tension began to twist in his gut. "Somebody from her classes?"

"No. It's Nick."

"Nick? Nick Barnes?" Jonas frowned thoughtfully, relieved somewhat. At least this was a situation he could control. The tension in his gut ebbed as his mind whirled.

He supposed he shouldn't be surprised that Nick had finally noticed Lynn was a lovely young woman. And Nick was certainly not hard to look at himself, so it shouldn't surprise him that Lynn might be interested in the handsome head of security.

"I'll handle that situation when I get back to the States," he said to Dunst. "Meanwhile you need to focus on our other project. I'll be back within the week and I hope you'll have some good news for me."

Jonas disconnected the call and sat on the edge of the king-size bed, his mind a jumble of thoughts. He knew he was under investigation by the FBI. He'd been under investigation ever since they tied him to drug smuggler Marshall Carrington. So far they hadn't been able to prove anything but he was definitely on their radar.

The FBI surveillance was also the reason he tried to be out of the States whenever Lynn was going to retrieve a treasure. He made sure he could never be tied to the theft of those precious items.

If the FBI interest wasn't enough, there was a possibility that James Whitlow wouldn't win his bid for re-election as president of the United States in November. Ever since that bitch reporter, Tory Patton, had done an exposé of Whitlow's questionable campaign money, Whitlow had lost the support of many of his constituents.

Jonas had donated a huge amount of money to Whitlow's campaign and had slipped in some funding from a drug lord he'd done business with in the past. That source of funds had created a blackmail tool that had put Jonas in the driver's seat. He'd been able to gently "persuade" the current administration to push legislation that was favorable to his interests.

If Whitlow lost the election in November, then Jonas would lose his power base in the White House. The thought of losing power was enough to put Jonas in a foul mood.

He got up from the bed and paced back and forth across the expanse of lush beige carpeting. The project Dunst was working on was to find a buyer for the diamond Lynn had lifted several days ago. Jonas was confident the sale would occur without a hitch.

Once again he stopped at the window and stared outside, where he could see in the distance the Eiffel Tower rising up against a cloudy sky. But his thoughts weren't on the pleasures of Paris.

He was worried about Lynn. Never had she questioned him about the work they did the way she had the other night. The intelligence she possessed that was such an asset just might eventually become a liability.

It wasn't just her intelligence he worried about. He'd always known that she would grow up, that she'd want a relationship with a man. He'd dreaded the moment that might occur, had known it would be the beginning of a loss of control for him.

At least according to Dunst it was Nick he had to worry about instead of a classmate or stranger that he knew nothing about.

He'd been thinking about bringing Nick into the fold, allowing him more responsibility, more access to the inner workings of his business dealings. Maybe now was the time for that.

Surely in the last couple of days Nick and Lynn hadn't developed a relationship so close that she would have told him about her special powers. He hoped his warnings to her from the time she was a mere toddler would keep her from sharing that particular information with anyone.

Lynn had always been malleable and trusting concerning the work Jonas had her doing. She believed that each time she "retrieved" an artifact or jewel she was doing something good and altruistic. He didn't want anything or anyone to change that.

Somehow he'd manage to deal with the questions she asked and assuage any doubts she might entertain about their work. She was his golden goose, stealing treasures and allowing him to fill his coffers with money. He would do and say whatever necessary to keep her working for him.

He smiled. Lynn had been his best, his finest acquisition.

If he found out that she'd told Nick about her work and about her unusual skills, and if Nick became a problem, then Jonas would do what was necessary to solve the problem.

Nick Barnes was expendable. If he wound up on the beach somewhere with a bullet in his head, the authorities would probably assume his murder had to do with his background, with the organized crime family he'd turned his back on.

Jonas left the window and walked over to the mini-bar, where he fixed himself a scotch on the rocks. He shouldn't be surprised that Lynn was testing her feminine wiles on a man. Jonas had been lucky she hadn't experienced any real, deep relationship in the past.

Maybe he should encourage this romance between her and Nick. At least Jonas could control the situation better if the suitor was Nick. Nick would have two choices. He could either go along with the program or he could wind up dead.

Chapter 5

Lynn stood at her bedroom window and looked out. The night was dark, with thick cloud cover obscuring any moonlight that might try to shine down to earth.

Perfect, she thought as she left the window. It was just after midnight and she was ready to leave. Clad in a black pair of tight stretch slacks and a long-sleeved black T-shirt, she grabbed the stocking cap and a backpack of equipment from her bed and left the room.

Adrenaline pumped through her as she silently made her way down the stairs. She knew Rita and Arturo would be sound asleep.

She slipped as soundlessly as a shadow through the house out the mudroom door, then hurried across the driveway to where her car awaited her. She was focused solely on the task ahead. Get in, get the vase and get out.

Moments later, as she drove toward the Markham Convention Center, her thoughts raced to the job ahead. There was much about her work that she didn't understand.

She hated feeling like a thief, but Jonas had assured her many times that these thefts were secretly sanctioned by the government. He'd told her that it was important that he remain as distant from their work as possible, that as a wealthy businessman he'd made political enemies that could make life difficult for him if it was discovered what he and Lynn did.

He had also explained to her countless times that the local authorities weren't aware of the government involvement, and if she were caught she would be treated like a common criminal until the appropriate authorities could be contacted. However, he'd always assured her that the worst she could expect was a couple of hours in jail cooling her heels.

This made her all the more careful in the planning stages of each retrieval. The last thing she wanted was to get caught, arrested and taken down to a jail cell even if she'd only be there until the matter could be resolved.

Besides, if she were honest with herself she'd have to confess that she loved the challenge of this work.

She loved using her natural skills and intelligence to do something few real thieves would even attempt.

It was a matter of pride that she not get caught and hauled into a police station like a common criminal.

The Markham Convention Center was one of several buildings in a block on the south side of Miami. The buildings were specifically used by large groups holding conventions or for special-interest groups holding exhibits open to the public.

Because normally the place was used for business conventions and not exclusively for exhibits, the security wasn't terrific. There were alarms at the doors and security guards who walked the perimeter, but that was it.

The exhibit going on now was advertised as Treasures from the Nile and touted as being one of the best collections of artifacts and archeological finds from Egypt.

Lynn had been to the Markham Convention Center often in the past. Whenever there was an exhibit of something she found interesting, she attended. During those frequent visits she'd gotten a good feel for the layout of the place, and that was vital for her plans this evening.

There was little traffic on the streets at midnight despite the fact that it was a Saturday night. It was too late for club-goers to be just arriving at clubs and far too early for them to be heading home.

She parked on a residential street three blocks from the convention center. There she left the car and started off on foot, the navy backpack slung over her shoulder and her stocking cap in her pocket.

The street she walked down was quiet, the houses dark while the occupants slept. Occasionally she'd see the flicker of dim lights and could imagine a couple in the house all cuddled up on the sofa watching a late-night movie on television.

What would it be like to have that kind of life? To have somebody beside you who cared about you, somebody who was there when you needed him? Not a godfather but a lover. That's what she often thought about in the dark hours of night when loneliness pressed so close against her.

She certainly wasn't going to find a romantic relationship through her e-mail or by surfing the Net. She was always conscious that those friendly relationships were built on a premise of anonymity. A person she thought to be a twenty-seven-year-old businessman could just as easily be a lonely ninety-year-old man or a hormone-driven teenager.

A block from her goal, she left the residential streets behind and walked behind a small strip mall. She would approach the convention center from the back.

She was guessing there would be no guards at the back of the building. A solid ten-foot-high concrete wall provided all the security needed at the back of the building.

At the front of the building there were two spotlights that shone day and night on the front facade, making a frontal attack dangerous. At the back there were no lights at all, and without moonlight it was a thick darkness that enveloped the area around the concrete wall.

Lynn crouched at the foot of the wall and used her acute hearing to assess her surroundings. Insects filled the air with night songs of clicking and buzzing, and in the distance a dog barked.

Lynn hoped there weren't any guard dogs in the convention center. She rarely encountered guard dogs and didn't want to ever encounter them again while doing this work.

Dogs scared her. It was a totally irrational fear, bred from a single incident that had occurred when she'd been ten years old. A friend of Jonas's had come to the house carrying his pet poodle in his arms. He'd put the dog down, and the poodle had taken one look at Lynn and run to her and bitten her on the ankle.

It hadn't been a bad bite, had barely broken the skin, but from that moment on Lynn had been frightened of dogs.

She placed her ear against the concrete wall. She heard no sniffing, no snorting, nor did she smell anything that would indicate there were guard dogs on the other side.

She stood and shrugged off the backpack. She pulled the stocking cap out of her pocket and pulled it on, hiding her hair beneath. Gloves came next, the thin latex kind that didn't impede movement but kept fingerprints from showing up.

She retrieved a penlight and Swiss Army knife from the backpack but ignored the rope and grappling hook. She would use those only if necessary.

She was hoping that by using the tremendous power in her legs she could spring to the top of the concrete wall without the aid of the hook and rope. She hid her backpack beneath a nearby bush, then returned to the wall.

Listening once again to make certain she heard no sounds that would portend trouble, she squatted, gathered her strength and sprang straight up the wall. Her hands grabbed the top of the wall and she hung for a moment, gathering her strength to pull herself up and over. One…two…three, she thought, then hoisted herself to the top.

The wall itself was about eighteen inches wide and four feet or so from the back of the building. She jumped to the ground below, once again crouching as she listened for anything amiss.

Just ahead of her on the back of the building was a vent cover. It was small, but not so tiny that she couldn't get through it. She knew from studying the plans for the building that the vent would lead into the mechanical room, the room that held the furnace, air conditioner and the hot water tanks. This was her way in.

Turning on her penlight, she shone it toward where she thought the vent should be. Sure enough, there it was, connected to the building by six Phillips screws. She pulled the Swiss Army knife from her pocket and shut off the penlight. Using her fingers to guide her, she carefully unfastened the screws and loosened the vent cover.

When she was finished, she replaced the knife in her pocket along with the screws, then once again pulled out her penlight. Shining it into the vent she saw that it was exactly what she'd been looking for. The vent led into a dark room where she could hear the hum of the air conditioner at work.

She slid through the vent without any problems and landed soundlessly on the floor inside. With her penlight she checked out her surroundings.

She was exactly where she wanted to be. A door was just ahead and she was pleased to see that it locked from the inside. Apparently the janitorial staff used keys to get in and out of here. Besides the furnace and water heaters, the room also held a small desk where apparently the janitors took their breaks and stole an occasional puff on a cigarette. She could smell the lingering scent of old tobacco.

The Markham Convention Center was comprised

of six different rooms besides the kitchen and various rest rooms. Each room had its own name. The owner of the Markham Convention Center had a thing for the golden years of Hollywood.

The largest room, the Bogart Room, was the one typically used for huge gatherings. Next to the Bogart Room was the Hepburn Room, another large area. Doors between these two rooms could be opened to create a space big enough to hold any group that might want to use this facility.

The smaller rooms, the Monroe, the Davis, the Crawford and the Gable were the ones usually used for the occasional exhibits. The Treasures from the Nile exhibit was taking place in the Gable room.

Lynn had been in that room several times for various displays and exhibitions. She unlocked the door that led out of the mechanical room and slipped a flat piece of metal out of her pocket.

Placing it against the lock mechanism, she went out into the hallway and allowed the door to close behind her, knowing the piece of metal would keep it from locking again. The last thing she wanted was to be locked out of her escape route.

The hall was dark, and she turned to the left, where the Gable Room was located. Once again she listened for any sound of human presence. The air conditioner was noisy, making it difficult to hear much of anything else, but she didn't sense anyone around.

Still, she kept her penlight off, knowing that somewhere in the building there would be at least one security guard. She didn't want a single, faint beam from the tiny light to give away her presence.

She smelled the air surrounding her, the scent a combination of floor wax and disinfectant and the odors of people who had passed through the hallway in the past twenty-four hours.

Using her hands to guide her, she made her way down the long, dark hallway and entered into a large lobby. Here, lights from the front entrance flickered in, giving the lobby a ghostly gray light. This is the place she'd be most vulnerable, as she crossed the lobby to get to the Gable Room.

Once again a burst of adrenaline rushed through her. Within minutes she would have the vase in hand and hopefully be back in her car and driving home. She could do this. This was the one thing she did well.

It was odd, but she felt as if somehow, by completing this job successfully, she would make up for both her indiscretion the night before in the club and not answering Jonas's phone calls to her that morning.

Focused on the opposite side of the lobby, she left the deep black of the hallway behind and started across.

"Freeze! FBI!" The deep male voice came from someplace on her left.

FBI?

She didn't freeze. She whirled on her heels and ran back the way she had come. Bang. Bang. Bang. Her heart crashed frantically, like bass drums thundering in her chest.

She raced back down the hallway toward the mechanical room. A flurry of activity and shouting came from behind her. Sheer panic ripped through her.

"Get him!"

"Go…go!"

Voices yelled from every direction.

Run! Run! A voice screamed in her head. She moved faster than she'd ever moved in her life. She'd just ducked into the mechanical room when she heard the unmistakable sound of a gunshot.

Guns. Bullets.

Fingers fumbling, she locked the door behind her and raced to the vent.

Her mind was numbed, in shock.

Get out.

Get out. The two words screamed in her head. Get out and get away. Panic constricted her lungs, making each breath painful.

She slithered through the vent and to the outside, vaguely aware of the sounds of bodies slamming against the locked door behind her in an effort to spring it open.

She hit the outside and jumped at the wall, nearly

sobbing with relief as her fingers gripped the top. In two seconds she'd pulled herself up and over.

She hit the ground on the other side, grabbed her backpack and ran for her life.

Lungs sucking air, feet pounding the pavement, she raced down the block, at any moment expecting the sound of pursuit or the whiz of a bullet speeding toward her.

Her head was devoid of any thoughts other than for her survival. By the time she reached her car she was out of breath and trembling uncontrollably. She slid in behind the steering wheel, yanked off the stocking cap and pulled off the gloves.

It took her three tries before she finally managed to get her key into the ignition.

Not too fast, she told herself as she pulled away from the curb. The last thing she wanted to do was draw any attention to herself as she left the area.

The trembling stopped within minutes of driving, but once she realized she was relatively safe, the events replayed in her head in horrifying detail.

When she felt she'd put enough distance between herself and the convention center, she pulled over to the curb, needing to pull herself together before continuing the drive home.

She'd been shot at! A shiver raced up her spine as she thought of how close she'd come to not only being caught, but to being killed or maimed.

They'd been waiting for her. And it hadn't been the local cops, it had been the FBI. What was the FBI doing there?

They'd shot at her, for God's sake. Jonas had always warned her that if she were caught on one of these work details, she'd be arrested and taken to jail until the appropriate authorities could arrange for her release. But nobody could arrange for a release if she was dead.

She drew deep, steadying breaths for several minutes, trying to still her trembling, the jagged nerves that roared through her. Finally she pulled away from the curb and headed home.

She had to talk to Jonas. Something wasn't right. She had to tell Jonas that the FBI had tried to kill her. Why had they been there? Surely they would know about the work she and Jonas did for the government.

By the time she got back to her house and was in her room, she was in a state of frenzy. She stripped off her clothes and buried them in the back of her closet, then pulled on a robe and sat on the edge of her bed.

At any moment she expected a knock on the door, an arrest warrant to be served. They had been waiting for her. How had they known that she'd attempt a heist tonight? And why were the FBI involved?

Maybe they'd been there to protect the display. It could be a coincidence.

She grabbed her cell phone and punched in the number to connect her to Jonas. His phone went directly to his voice mail.

"Uncle Jonas. Call me as soon as possible." She disconnected and threw the phone aside. Nervous energy raged inside her, and she stalked over to the window and peered outside.

For the past couple of months the questions about the work she did had been growing bigger and bigger in her head. The answers Jonas had given her the other night when she'd asked some of those questions hadn't really satisfied her, but because she loved Jonas, because she trusted him, she hadn't pushed too hard.

She stared out the window where the clouds still obscured the stars and the moon. The only lights shining were the ones for security purposes on the property.

She leaned her forehead against the glass windowpane and wondered if Nick was working. She doubted it. He'd mentioned that he was on duty at noon today. By now he'd be home.

The fear that had chased her home was dissipating, leaving in its wake only confusion. How she wished she had somebody to talk to, somebody other than Jonas.

Somebody like Nick. But of course she couldn't talk to him about what had happened tonight. Even though he'd rescued her from her own stupidity at the club, she didn't know him well enough to tell him her secrets. She didn't trust him enough to tell him about her work, about herself.

She'd been lonely all her life, but at this moment she felt more isolated and alone than she'd ever felt in her entire life.

The phone rang and she whirled from the window and grabbed it from the bed. "I went after the vase tonight and the FBI was there waiting for me. They even shot at me. I could have been killed." The fear that had momentarily quieted now shouted from her. "Why was the FBI there? You always told me that all I had to worry about was local cops and security guards."

"Slow down, Lynn. Take a breath," Jonas said calmly.

His calm only fed the flames of her anxiety. "Take a breath? I was almost killed tonight. Didn't you hear what I told you? They shot at me."

"Calm down, Lynn." She drew a deep breath, at the same time sitting on the edge of her bed. "Now, first of all, I'm assuming you aren't hurt or in jail."

"No, I managed to escape."

"Did anyone get a good look at you?"

She frowned thoughtfully. "I don't think so. As I was running, I heard somebody shout, 'Get him,' which means they didn't realize I was female."

"Did you get the vase?"

The question irritated her. "I barely got out with my skin intact. No, I didn't get the vase. They were on to me the minute I stepped into the lobby. Since when is the FBI involved in all this?"

Jonas was silent for a long moment. "I don't know," he finally said thoughtfully. "There must have been a breakdown in communication somewhere. The Feds shouldn't have been involved in this at all."

"Yeah, well, they were. I want to talk to your contact. I want to know exactly what happened tonight that almost got me killed."

"Calm down, dear. We'll discuss all this further when I get home. I'll talk to my contact and see if I can get some answers. In the meantime, perhaps we should lay low until this is all resolved."

"Trust me, I don't intend to try another recovery until I know you have things under control at your end."

"I'll make some phone calls and see what's going on. You might want to think back and see what you might have missed when you went in."

Lynn frowned thoughtfully. Had she missed something? "When will you be home?"

"I won't be there until Monday or Tuesday. In the meantime, I understand you've been dating Nick."

It took a moment for her to follow the jump in topic. "So, Richard is doing double duty, not only working as your partner but also as your spy." She heard the edge in her voice and knew if she weren't so upset she'd never use that tone with her godfather. "For your information, I'm not dating Nick. We just went for a drive together this morning. It was no big deal."

"He's a good man, Lynn. The idea of seeing two people I care about getting together certainly doesn't upset me."

The night was filled with surprises. She never would have expected this kind of reaction from Jonas, who'd always cautioned her about dating and getting too close to any one person.

"Of course, I would expect you to be circumspect about sharing with Nick anything about our work or your particular skills," Jonas continued.

"Of course," she replied, and stretched out on the bed. Now that the fear had been spent and her anger vented, she was exhausted.

She didn't want to think about Nick, or her work, or anything else. At the moment she just wanted to drift into sleep and put this nightmarish night behind her.

"Lynn, honey. Don't worry. I'll get everything straightened out and we'll discuss it all when I get home. In the meantime you just relax and enjoy the next couple of days."

"All right," she agreed.

"And remember, baby, that I love you."

"I love you, too, Uncle Jonas."

The minute they hung up Lynn shut off her light and crawled beneath the covers on her bed. Sleep was a long time coming.

She'd been doing recovery work for Jonas for almost two years. In total, she'd recovered about fifteen items. In all of those fifteen times she'd never been accosted by anyone, never been seen at all.

Had she done something to screw up tonight? Had she not listened carefully enough? Had she been arrogantly reckless? She didn't think so, but now she wasn't sure. Had she been thinking about Nick and not focused enough on the job?

There was no way she could have known those agents were waiting for her. But was it possible her mind had wandered for a moment and she'd missed a sound, a scent that should have alerted her?

Once again she was struck by the illogical elements where her work was concerned. If the FBI had somehow become aware of the "robberies" she'd committed, then they would have to know that the items she'd been stealing were stolen. Why didn't they just get the items themselves and return them to their rightful owners?

Jonas's vague explanations of the craziness of politics and the work having to be carried out by a secret, covert agency just didn't ring true.

But if she believed Jonas was lying to her about the

work, then she'd have to wonder what else he might be lying to her about.

These were crazy thoughts. Of course he wasn't lying to her. He was the one constant in her life, the one person she'd always looked up to, depended on. She couldn't imagine a reason for him to lie to her about anything.

It was almost noon when she awakened the next day. Whatever clouds had possessed the night had long ago burned away as brilliant sunshine streamed in through her window.

Relax. That's what Jonas had told her to do for the next couple of days. Maybe she'd meet Vicki for lunch. She felt the need to connect with somebody wonderfully normal. A brief phone call to Vicki let her know lunch wasn't possible.

The pool. It had been over a week since she'd swum, and maybe the physical exercise would still the restless energy that had possessed her since she'd opened her eyes a few minute ago.

By one o'clock she was on her way out to the cabana. The Olympic-size pool beckoned to her as she walked past it and into the cabana, where she'd find everything she needed for swimming.

Moments later, clad in her one-piece swimsuit, she dove into the water and began to swim laps. The temperature of the water was perfect, and Lynn had always enjoyed swimming.

She swam the length of the pool with powerful strokes, did a tumble and swam back. Her mind was blessedly empty as she cut through the water. She did twenty laps, then pulled herself up and sat on the edge of the pool.

"Exorcising demons?"

The deep, familiar voice came from behind her, and she whirled around to see Nick standing just outside the pool area. Despite everything that weighed heavily on her mind, the sight of him caused a shiver of utter feminine pleasure to sweep over her.

Clad in a pair of tight jeans and a white T-shirt, he looked casually rugged and masculine.

"No demons, just getting a little workout." She was grateful her towel was nearby and grabbed it to her chest as he stepped closer.

She felt the heat of his gaze as it swept over her scantily clad body. She felt danger as clearly as she had the night before, but this was a delicious kind of danger. She stood, keeping the towel in front of her as if to shield her from the provocative heat of his eyes.

"No Alabama Slammers poolside?" he teased.

She winced. "No more Alabama Slammers for the rest of my life."

He laughed. "There's nothing wrong with cutting loose occasionally, as long as you're among good friends. And you were."

"Yes, they are good friends," she agreed.

"Have dinner with me, Lynn. Tonight. Let's have dinner and go dancing," he said.

"All right," she said without hesitation.

"Good. Why don't I pick you up around seven?"

"That would be fine. I'll be ready."

He nodded and she watched him as he walked away.

Funny, yesterday she'd wanted her work to take her mind off Nick. Now she hoped being with Nick would keep her mind off work and the doubts about certain things Jonas had told her.

Chapter 6

Time crept by for the remainder of the afternoon as Lynn anticipated her date with Nick. At least she didn't have to worry about Jonas's disapproval of her plans for the night. He'd all but given his blessing for her to see Nick.

At quarter to seven she stood in front of her mirror and gazed at her reflection. She had chosen a black-and-red knee-length Valentino dress she'd never worn before. She was pleased to see that the fit was perfect. She looked chic and sexy.

Thankfully the nerves that thrummed inside her weren't outwardly evident. She turned away from the mirror and picked up her cell phone and her purse. She started to tuck the phone into her purse, then changed her mind and instead tossed it into the dresser drawer in her nightstand.

She would not be bothered with phone calls tonight.

At five to seven she went downstairs to await Nick's arrival. She went into the living room and sat on the burgundy leather sofa. Within seconds the paintings on the walls turned from the Picassos Jonas loved to display to several Monet watercolors that were Lynn's favorites. Of course, when they were both in the room, the Picassos remained. Jonas was master of the house.

She rarely paid much attention to the technology that Jonas loved, but tonight it irritated her. She didn't like the idea of sensors being able to track her movements through the house even if only for the benign reason of attending to her personal comfort levels.

She wondered what Jonas would do if she told him she wanted to move out, to get a place of her own. In truth she didn't have to wonder. She knew he'd blow a fuse.

He'd tell her it was ridiculous to move out of a house in which, other than the help, she was often the sole occupant. He'd warn her about kidnapping plots and personal danger as he always did when it came to her stretching her wings in any way.

But no one had ever attempted to kidnap her. Jonas had kept her like a treasure under glass, but she was beginning to wonder if she were a treasure wanted by anyone other than Jonas.

Lately she'd thought a lot about what it would be like to have her own little place, a place where her friends could gather, a place where she would feel competent and in control of her surroundings.

The ring of the doorbell pulled her from her thoughts, and a new surge of nervous tension filled her. "I'll get it," she called out for Rita's benefit. She went to the door and pulled it open.

Nick looked more handsome than she'd ever seen him. He wore a pair of black slacks and a dark gray dress shirt, but it wasn't his choice of clothing that she found so appealing. Rather it was that look in his eyes, the appreciative look of a male for a female he found attractive.

She had a feeling it was going to be a night to remember.

"You look amazing," he said, and held out his hand for hers.

"Thank you." She slipped her hand into his and allowed him to draw her out of the house and toward his car. It was a perfect evening, warm but with a faint breeze that kept it from being too warm. To Lynn it felt like an evening filled with romantic possibility, and all her senses were alive with a simmering excitement.

"Where are we going?" she asked once they were in the car and were headed down the highway.

"A favorite place of mine. The food is terrific, the dance floor is small, and the music is slow."

How was it possible that with a single sentence he could spark a fire in the pit of her stomach? "Sounds wonderful," she murmured.

Not only did the plans for the evening sound wonderful, but Nick smelled wonderful. He wore a woodsy cologne that filled the interior of the car, which, coupled with the fainter scent of a menthol shaving cream, was boldly masculine.

"Beautiful night, isn't it?" he asked.

She smiled. "I was just thinking the same thing."

"Have you heard from Jonas since he's been gone?"

"Yes, he's in Paris. I spoke to him last night. He's planning on coming home in the next day or two." She hesitated a moment, then continued. "I'm thinking about telling him when he gets back that I want to get my own place."

Nick looked at her, his dark eyebrows raised in surprise. "Really? Have you been thinking about moving out for a while?"

She frowned thoughtfully. "It's crossed my mind off and on for the past year, but lately I've been thinking about it a lot. I adore Uncle Jonas, but he treats me like a baby, and I'm not a baby."

His gaze slid to her face, then down the length of her. "No, you definitely aren't a baby," he agreed dryly.

The man should have those looks bottled, she thought. He could sell them as sheer sex appeal. She fought to regain her composure. "Where do you live, Nick?"

"I've got a one-bedroom apartment at the Heritage Arms."

The Heritage Arms was a luxury apartment building not far from where she lived. "It must be nice to have your own space, be surrounded by your own things and be able to come and go as you please without feeling as if you're being watched all the time."

"When Jonas is out of town, you pretty much have the house to yourself," he countered as he made a right turn onto a coastal road.

"True," she agreed. "But it's Jonas's house and of course Rita and Arturo are always there."

"Yeah, but if you move out won't you miss all the bells and whistles you have at home now?"

"Not a bit," she replied. "I don't care a thing about those bells and whistles." She thought of all the technology Jonas was so proud of, technology she found intrusive.

He cast her a quick sideways glance. "What do you plan to do when you graduate?"

"I'd like to work for Uncle Jonas. I'm hoping once I finish school he'll bring me into the business and make me a more active partner in his import/export work. I keep most of his financial records for him, but I'd like to do more."

"No desire to strike out on your own? Build something that's just yours?"

"Certainly I want to have a life of my own. I like dabbling in developing video games, but I'd be a fool to turn my back on the opportunity of working with Uncle Jonas. Besides the import business, he does such important work with the government, and I'd love to be a part of all that." She slid him a glance. "Isn't that why you're working for Uncle Jonas?"

"Sure. I'll admit it. I want to do more than work for Jonas. I want to work with him."

"Sounds like we both have a common goal." She flashed him a challenging look.

He laughed, his straight white teeth flashing in the illumination from the dashboard. "I'd say there's room for two at the top, don't you think?"

"Is that why you invited me out? Why you've taken an interest in me? To advance your career with Uncle Jonas?"

He sighed with obvious impatience. "I told you the other day that has nothing to do with it. I'll tell you why I took an interest in you, Lynn."

He didn't look at her but instead kept his focus on the road ahead. "I took an interest in you because for the first time the other night I realized how silky your hair looked. I noticed when you smile your mouth looks like it needs to be kissed badly, and I realized I wanted to be the man to do it."

"Do you always do this?" she asked, her heart beating a little faster at his words.

"Do what?"

"Seduce a woman with words before you've even eaten dinner with her?" Lynn felt her cheeks burn with a blush at her own boldness. But something about Nick made her feel reckless and bold.

"Would you prefer I wait until after we eat?"

"No…I mean, I'm not sure. I don't think I've ever really been seduced before."

"Really?" Once again he looked at her in surprise, then grinned that bold, sexy smile. "Then I'll have to make sure and do it right."

That seemed to set the tone for the evening. He took her to a place called Smokey's, a small club that catered to an older crowd and was located on the waterfront.

The interior was semidark, the dance floor small and the tables spaced to provide maximum privacy to all of the diners.

Nick placed a hand in the small of her back as they were led to their table near the dance floor, where several couples swayed to an old standard tune being played by a quartet. She felt the burn of his touch through the fabric of her dress.

They were left alone to peruse small menus. "How

did you ever find this place?" she asked as she opened her menu.

"My parents used to come here when I was younger. We had a lot of family gatherings here. They all stopped coming a long time ago, but I occasionally drop in for dinner or a drink. I like the old music and the ambiance."

She wondered if by coming here he felt some sort of connection to the family who had disowned him. Her heart softened with empathy for him. What must it be like to have a father who had cut you out firmly and forever from his life? What kind of scars did that leave behind?

The waitress arrived to take their orders. "The house specialty is seafood, but they also make a mean steak," Nick said. He ordered a steak and baked potato, while Lynn decided on shrimp with wild rice, and they both ordered a glass of wine.

"So, you don't do the club scene?" she asked when the waitress had departed.

"Not much. To tell the truth, for the last couple of years I haven't had much time for socializing. I've been too focused on work. But you know what they say about all work and no play." His dark eyes gleamed in the light of the candle that flickered in the center of their table.

"I can't imagine anything making you boring. I'm the boring one with no life outside of school."

"There's a difference between being boring and being a bit naive. From what I've heard about your up-bringing, you've just been sheltered, that's all."

Sheltered. She was naive and sheltered, but she'd been shot at by an FBI agent the night before. She shoved this thought away, not wanting to ruin the evening with Nick by dwelling on what had happened the night before.

"Maybe I should have remained sheltered, considering what a fool I made of myself at Sensations," she said dryly.

He laughed. "It's not an uncommon phenomenon that young women who have never really been free tend to overimbibe when they get a taste of freedom."

"I'll keep that in mind for the future."

Their dinner arrived, and as they ate they talked. It was a conversation of discovery. They spoke about favorite foods, movies they'd seen and politics. It was the kind of talk that began the path to knowledge about each other, the path that led to the first step in intimacy.

There wasn't a moment during the conversation that Lynn didn't know he was subtly seducing her. The seduction was there in his dark eyes each time he looked at her, there in the frequency of his touch to her hand when he wanted to make a point.

It was a heady experience for Lynn. She'd had men come on to her before, but never with the smoothness or the breathtaking intensity of Nick. It both excited her and made her wary. Her isolated lifestyle and unusual senses had kept her from acting on an attraction to a man so far. Perhaps it was time to take a chance.

There was no getting around it: she was hungry for a relationship. Not so hungry that she'd settle for a smooth-talking man with lust in his eyes and nothing else on the table. She wasn't a fool.

But she found Nick easy to talk to. The shyness that normally plagued her seemed to disappear with him.

They ate at a leisurely pace, as if they had all the time in the world to enjoy each other's company.

When they'd finished eating, he got them each another glass of wine, then gestured toward the dance floor. "Ready for a spin?"

The music was soft, romantic, and the thought of being held in his arms thrilled her more than just a little. "I'm game if you are, although I can't promise I won't step on your toes."

"I think I can handle that." He rose and held out his hand to her.

She had a feeling he could handle anything. She hadn't forgotten the look in his eyes that night in the bar when he'd looked around for the creep who had backed her into a corner. Nor had she missed the way his gaze had swept the room when they'd first walked in here tonight. It had been the watchful gaze of a man with secrets.

There was something slightly dark, slightly dangerous about Nick Barnes. She wondered if perhaps it
had something to do with his family. All she knew for
sure was that he intrigued her.

He led her to the dance floor and pulled her into
his arms. He didn't hold her so close as to be offen-
sive, but close enough that she felt the inviting heat
from his body, the warmth of his breath on the top of
her head and the strength of his arm around her back.

She had a perfect view of his jawline and the hollow of his throat. His skin looked soft, and for a moment she wondered what it would be like to press her
lips against it. The idea of kissing him electrified her.

He was a good dancer. He didn't just stand in place
and sway, but rather moved them around the floor
with an easy masculine grace, using his hand in the
small of her back to guide her.

He looked down at her. "So far so good. No
crushed toes."

She smiled. "You make it easy to stay off your
toes. You're a good lead."

He tightened his arm around her and pulled her a
bit closer. She could now feel his hard chest against
her breasts, feel his muscled thighs against her own.
A wave of warmth swept through her.

"So, what's Jonas doing in Paris?" he asked as they
continued to move to the music.

"I'm not sure. He goes there pretty frequently." In

fact, that's usually where he was when she did a recovery for him.

"Does he have business interests over there?"

"You know Uncle Jonas. He has business dealings everywhere."

"There's still a lot about his work that I don't know."

Lynn said nothing. There was a lot about *her* that Nick didn't know. She wondered if she would ever be close enough, ever feel safe enough to share with somebody the secret of her amazing physical skills. Would she ever be able to share the details of the work she did for Jonas? Would she ever find somebody with whom she could share all the pieces of herself without being afraid?

"What's this government work he does? He's never mentioned that to me before," Nick asked.

"I don't know much about it. I just know he has defense contracts with the government, but he keeps that business separate from the import/export business."

When the song ended, they returned to their table and made small talk while they each finished their glass of wine. They danced two more dances, then left.

As they were walking toward the car, Lynn noticed how beautiful the beach looked behind the restaurant. The moon was a plump round ball that shot shimmering silver across the ocean waves and the sandy beach.

"Look, Nick. Isn't it beautiful?"

"Want to take a walk?" He looked down at her high heels. "Never mind, bad idea."

"On the contrary." She walked to the edge of the sand and kicked off her shoes. "I'd love to take a walk."

He grinned at her, that slow sexy grin that stole her breath. He took off his shoes and socks, and together they walked on the still-warm sand.

As they walked, he reached for her hand. "I can't imagine living anywhere else, can you?"

She shook her head. "I've traveled to so many places, seen some beautiful countries, but Miami is my home and I love it here."

"I know you like to swim, but do you enjoy other water sports? Boating? Surfing?"

"I've never tried to surf, but I enjoy being on the water. What about you? Do you surf?"

"Whenever I get a chance," he replied.

Her mind filled with a vision of him in a bathing suit, balancing on a surfboard as it flew across the waves. "I'll bet you're good at it."

His dark eyes gleamed in the moon's illumination. "I try to be good at everything I do."

"I'm sure you do," she murmured. She broke the eye contact and instead gazed out at the water. "I'd love to have a place right on the beach."

"Jonas's place is on the beach," he countered.

"Yes, and it's always been home. But now I'd like my own place. I'd like just a little cottage where nobody knows who I am, where nobody could find me unless I want them to."

They walked several steps in silence. "I have a place like that," he finally said.

She looked at him in surprise. "But I thought you said you lived in an apartment at the Heritage Arms."

"I do, but I've also got a beach house down on Harbor Road. It's just a little two-bedroom cottage that I'm renting with the option to buy. I don't get to spend as much time as I'd like there, but it's my little getaway from the world."

"Sounds marvelous," she said.

"The house number is 215. The key is under a flowerpot on the front porch. You're welcome to use it whenever you want."

The offer was unexpected, and so generous that she was momentarily at a loss for words. She squeezed his hand. "Thank you, that's very kind of you."

He shrugged. "Most of the time it just sits there empty."

They continued to walk in a pleasant silence. A balmy breeze blew off the water, and the rhythmic rush of wave to shore was intoxicating.

"I'm so glad I left the cell phone at home," she said, finally breaking the silence.

"Won't your uncle wonder where you are and who you might be with?"

"I think he'll guess who I'm with. Richard must have mentioned something about seeing the two of us together yesterday morning because Jonas asked if we were seeing each other when I spoke to him this morning."

She felt the sudden tension that filled him. "What did you tell him?" he asked. "He isn't going to take me out to the swamp and feed me to the 'gators, is he?"

She laughed. "No, nothing like that. I told him that we'd gone for a drive together and it wasn't a big deal. Uncle Jonas likes you."

He stopped walking and turned to face her. "How do you know that?"

"Because he gave his approval about me seeing you."

"Let me tell you something, Lynn." That dangerous look shone from his eyes, transforming their dark depths to an almost silvery sheen in the moonlight. "If I wanted to see you I wouldn't give a damn whether your uncle gave his approval or not. I respect and admire your uncle, and I hope to work with him for a long time to come, but there are times when a man has to go after what he wants and damn the consequences."

There was a passion in his eyes, a dangerous light

of a man who always went after what he wanted and got it. It was that kind of passion she hungered for, the balancing without a net, the taking chances with your life, the reaching out for what you wanted without fear of failure or pain.

He squeezed her hand. "Sorry, I didn't mean to get so carried away."

"It's all right."

"We'd better get you home. Don't you have classes tomorrow?"

"Yes, I do," she said reluctantly. She didn't want to see the evening end.

They started walking again, back toward the car. Lynn was vaguely disappointed that he hadn't tried to kiss her. The setting, with the moonlight and the beach, had been so perfect for a romantic kiss.

She scoffed at the thought. She hadn't realized she had the heart of a romantic until this moment.

As they drove home Nick asked her about the many foreign places she'd visited in the past with Jonas. "We traveled a lot when I was younger," she said. "We'd fly to Paris or London, spend time in Switzerland and the Bahamas. We often went to Puerto Isla for visits. You name it and I've probably been there."

"Puerto Isla?"

"It's in Central America."

"Do you enjoy traveling?" he asked.

"I did when I was little, but not so much anymore.

Uncle Jonas seems to thrive on the jet-setting lifestyle, on never being in one place for too long. But I'm tired of it all. I like the idea of sticking in one place and building something permanent."

"I've never done much foreign traveling, but I've never had a big desire to," he said. "Like I said before, I love Miami."

All too soon he pulled up in front of the house. Again she thought of how much she hated to see the night come to an end. It had been one of the best nights she could ever remember.

Together they got out and walked toward the house. When they reached the door she turned to face him. "Thank you, Nick. I had a wonderful time."

"So did I." He reached up and brushed a strand of her hair back from her face. "I'd like to see you again, Lynn."

A flush of pleasure washed over her. "I'd like that."

"How about tomorrow night?"

She laughed a little breathlessly. "You don't let much grass grow under your feet."

"Not when it's something I care about." He leaned closer to her. "Remember what I said about your lips? That they looked like they needed kissing badly?"

"I remember." She felt as if she was scarcely breathing.

"They're looking like that right now."

"Then maybe you should kiss them."

He dipped his head and captured her mouth with his. Initially it was a soft kiss, the mere meeting of lips. But within seconds it transformed into something more, something deeper as she opened her mouth to him.

His arms wound around her, pulling her tight against him, so tight she could feel the press of his thighs and the hint of his arousal against her. His tongue swirled with hers and she felt herself burning from the inside out.

Before she combusted into fiery flames, he released her. "I don't know how well you do anything else, but you do that extremely well," she said unsteadily, then blushed.

He laughed, a low, sexy chuckle. "Can I call you tomorrow?" She nodded. "Then I'll just say goodnight for now."

"Good night, Nick." She watched as he left the porch and returned to his car. She touched her lips with two fingers, the feel of his mouth still imprinted there.

Lynn had been kissed before, more than a couple of times by several different men, but none of them had affected her like Nick had. He made her want more.

She stood on the porch until his car disappeared from view, then turned to go inside. As she reached for the doorknob she heard the faint crackling of brush nearby.

"Hello?" she called out. "Is somebody there?" She frowned and took a couple of steps away from the door. She tilted her head and listened, a wave of apprehension sweeping over her.

She could have sworn she heard footsteps…or had she? She allowed herself to listen. A breeze rustled the trees. Insects clicked and chirped. Nothing out of the ordinary. Maybe it had been a stray cat or a raccoon. "Is anyone there?" she called again. Nothing.

She went inside and locked the door behind her, her thoughts going back to Nick.

She liked him. What's more, she instinctively trusted him. Maybe it was because he worked for Jonas that trust had come so easily. Or maybe it was because he seemed to really listen to her, to ask questions that made her feel as if he was genuinely interested in her thoughts.

Whatever the reason, he excited her and she looked forward to spending more time with him. This was so much better than computer relationships, so much more real.

She went up to her room, drawn to her window by the stream of moonlight dancing in through the glass. She still tasted his kiss, felt the texture of his lips imprinted on her own. She'd wanted more…still did.

She froze as her gaze caught on a moving shadow. In the distance…in the trees. It was there only a moment, then gone. Or had it been there at all? She blinked and focused but saw nothing amiss.

Had she imagined it? Had her encounter the night before with the FBI made her imagine moving shadows and rustling leaves?

She turned away from the window, certain that if anyone who didn't belong had gotten on the property, security would have seen and responded.

Still, it was a very long time before she allowed herself to sleep that night.

Chapter 7

"It's been over two weeks, Nick. Surely you've learned something we can use." Ray's voice held more than a touch of impatience.

Nick fought back a sigh. "And I've seen her every night, but these things take time, Ray. If I ask too many pointed questions, she'll get suspicious and clam up altogether."

"A young woman like Lynn who has been so sheltered and isolated, I figured you could get beneath her defenses in no time."

"She's young and naive, but she isn't stupid, and she certainly isn't loose-lipped when she talks about Jonas."

"Our sources tell us he's out of the country again," Ray said.

"He is. According to Lynn he's in Rome arranging for the import of some unusual vases and glasses he found. He left yesterday."

"That's funny. Our information has him currently in Cuba."

Nick frowned. "What's he doing in Cuba?"

"Wish the hell we knew."

Nick leaned back his chair. "Look, Ray, I don't know what to tell you. If I push too hard, not only will I chase her off and we won't get anything from her, but I might jeopardize my job with Jonas, as well. I did manage to learn that she thinks he does some kind of defense contracting with the government."

"Yeah, right, and I'm the Easter Bunny," Ray said dryly.

"And I already told you that she does a lot of the bookkeeping. If evidence is there of his illegal activities, she'll have it."

"The evidence is there all right. It's just a matter of us getting our hands on those records. Turning her to our side would definitely be beneficial."

Nick frowned. "I agree, but trust me, that's not likely. She loves the man. You have to remember, Jonas is all the family Lynn knows." Nick sighed. "Look, Ray, I'll get what we need, you just have to give me a little more time."

"I know, I know." Ray's voice held the weight of the world. "I'm just getting tired of waiting, Nick. We've been after this guy for over two years and we don't seem any closer to putting him away now than we were when he first hit our radar."

"I'm doing the best I can," Nick replied. "I'm seeing her again this evening. I'll try to push a little harder for something we can use. I'll report in tomorrow morning."

Nick hung up and walked out onto the back deck of his cottage, irritated not just with the not-so-subtle push from his supervisor for results, but also by his own conflicted emotions where Lynn was concerned.

What had begun as an uncomplicated goal of seduction had, over the past two weeks, suddenly become complicated. The complication was the fact that he didn't want to seduce her completely. He didn't want to take her to bed with the intention of winning her trust and gaining her confidence to get Jonas behind bars.

He wanted to take her to bed for all the wrong reasons. He wanted to take her to bed because she smelled like lush summer flowers and her touch lit a flame in his gut. He wanted to take her to his bed to further explore the satin softness of her skin and hear moans of pleasure escaping her lips.

He wanted her, and that worried him.

Over the course of the past two weeks he'd gotten

to know her better and had come to recognize her relative innocence. He didn't want to be the one to introduce her to lovemaking, knowing that it was part of his job and his own desire but without promises of anything lasting. She deserved better than that.

He'd decided to continue a psychological seduction, but had also made up his mind that he would not attempt to take her to bed. Even this felt wrong, but it couldn't be helped.

He liked her—a lot—and he hadn't expected to. But he'd come to look forward to seeing her, to spending time with her, to sharing thoughts with her and hearing everything she thought about.

Dammit, he didn't want to like her, but he found himself drawn to her in a way that he hadn't been drawn to a woman in a very long time.

He walked back into the house and grabbed a beer from the refrigerator, recognizing that he'd never been so conflicted about doing a job. Something about Lynn White got to him. Something about her touched soft places Nick had forgotten still remained in his heart.

She continued to surprise him, as well. He hadn't expected the inner strength he occasionally saw flash from her eyes, hadn't expected the keen intelligence she possessed.

He returned to the patio, popped the top of his beer and checked his wristwatch. She'd be here in an hour.

He'd invited her to his little beachfront cottage for a quiet dinner.

Although he knew he'd taken a chance telling her about this secret place, he'd decided the risk might be worth the result. Getting her not only away from Jonas's house, but also out of a public area might make her relax enough to talk more openly about Jonas and his business.

He didn't believe Lynn knew anything about her godfather's illegal activities, but little pieces of information she gave him confirmed much of what the Bureau already knew.

As his financial bookkeeper she knew where Jonas's vast ill-gotten fortune was stashed, but she appeared to be certain that Jonas's fortune had been gained from his import/export business and Defense Department contracts that Nick knew didn't exist.

The information that she and Jonas had spent a lot of time in Puerto Isla had also not come as a surprise. The Bureau had already tied Jonas to a powerful drug lord in that small Central-American country.

He'd like to turn her, to get her on their side and have her help in bringing down the man who had raised her, but he knew that was impossible. Part of her charm was her unswerving devotion, her loyalty and love for Jonas White.

He took a drink of the beer and settled back in the deck chair. He had a few minutes before he had to start the charcoal for the steaks and throw together a salad.

Also weighing heavily on his mind was the most recent attempted robbery at the Markham Convention Center, which should have resulted in an arrest.

Although Nick hadn't been present at the convention center when the botched robbery attempt had gone down, the officers who had been there had reported to Ray that the suspect had been like a superhuman phantom. The perpetrator had run at the speed of light and had leaped over a concrete wall that nobody should have been able to jump over.

They'd had the culprit almost in the palm of their hands and yet he'd managed to escape their little net.

They knew Jonas was tied to the robberies, knew that he had sold several of the stolen items on the black market. But knowing and proving beyond a reasonable doubt were two different things. What they had to figure out was who worked as Jonas's agent. Who was doing the actual robberies?

Certainly it wasn't Dunst—although the man was mentally capable of anything, he didn't have the physical skills necessary to accomplish what the thief had done.

Nick suspected somebody on Jonas's payroll was their thief, but he had yet to identify who exactly that might be.

He had to consider everyone, even Lynn. Perhaps her late-night drives and talk of insomnia were just a cover.

It was difficult for him to believe that she'd have anything to do with the thefts. As far as he could discern, Lynn didn't have a criminal bone in her body. And Jonas had men on his payroll who had the backgrounds, the temperaments, the records of real criminals.

But he had to consider the possibility.

He'd just finished the last swallow of his beer and was about to get up when his phone rang once again.

The caller ID let him know it was his brother. It had been months since he'd heard from him. He steeled himself as he answered. "Anthony, what's up?"

"The old man wants to see you."

Nick couldn't have been more surprised if his brother had told him he'd just personally given birth to twins. It had been years since Nick's father had even acknowledged he was alive. "Yeah, well I'm not interested in seeing him."

"He's ill, Nick."

"Then tell him to call a doctor," he replied.

"Too late for that. It's cancer, Nick. He doesn't have much time left. He wants to see you again before it's too late."

Nick's chest tightened. He closed his eyes, unsure what he felt, what to do.

He'd long ago resigned himself to the fact that he was a man without a family, without a past. As far as he was concerned, his real life had begun when he had joined the Bureau.

He'd believed he was at peace until this moment, when the past reached out to grab him.

"Nick, you there?"

He opened his eyes as a sigh escaped him. "I'm here." He rubbed the center of his forehead where a headache began to throb. The knot in his chest constricted tightly.

He wanted to hang up the phone, stay away from the poisonous grip of his family, but instead heard himself saying, "Tell him tomorrow night. I'll come to the house around seven."

"Good. He'll be pleased." Without another word Anthony hung up.

Nick clicked off and stared out at the ocean waves. He rubbed his forehead once again and thought about downing another beer but decided against it. No amount of beer would lift away the chunk of stone that sat heavily on top of his heart.

Perhaps part of the problem with Lynn was that he could empathize with her too well. For years he'd seen the evidence of the kind of man his father was, the kinds of crimes he had committed. He'd seen the kind of men his father surrounded himself with, but he'd been too blind or just plain unwilling to recognize what he saw.

His awakening to who and what his father was had been excruciatingly painful. He'd had to face the fact that his life with his father had been built on broken trust, lies and manipulation.

He was surprised by how much he hated that eventually Lynn would have the same kind of awakening where Jonas was concerned and she, too, would know the kind of pain Nick had experienced.

Nick had never gotten emotionally involved with anyone on a case before in his life, but Lynn was getting under his skin. He'd have to walk a fine line. He needed to get what he could from her to help them build a case against her godfather. He had to be an active participant in destroying her life and he had to not care that that was what he was doing.

With another deep sigh he got up to start the charcoal.

Lynn drove the beachfront road slowly, looking for the address to Nick's cottage. It had been a strange and unsettling two weeks for her.

Jonas had returned to the States, but there had been a strain between them. He'd seemed cool, and she knew he'd been disappointed by her failure to retrieve the gold vase he'd wanted from the exhibit.

He'd assured her that he'd spoken to his contact, who had confirmed that a screw-up had occurred with the FBI involvement that night. He'd also mentioned another artifact he'd like recovered, a jeweled urn in the same exhibit as the gold vase.

"But I certainly don't expect you to handle it, Lynn," he'd said. "I just don't think you're up to it."

Those words had haunted her for the past two weeks. Her unusual physical skills had been the one thing she could always count on, the one gift she used to repay her godfather for taking her in and raising her like his own daughter. The fact that he'd lost faith in her and her abilities weighed heavily on her heart.

She had to believe that he was telling her the truth, that there had been a glitch with his contact and it had all been straightened out. She couldn't imagine any reason for Jonas to lie to her. As far as she knew, he'd never lied to her in the past.

He'd left again for another trip the day before and although everything had seemed okay between them when he'd told her goodbye, she'd felt a distance that had never been there before.

At that moment she had decided to go in for the urn and surprise him when he returned home again. The decision wasn't just for him alone. She needed to prove to herself that her skills were as sharp as they'd ever been and she could still depend on them.

Besides, that wasn't the only decision she'd made over the past two weeks. She would present Jonas not just with the urn, but also with the vase, then she would tell him that she was moving out.

It was time for her to build a life separate from her godfather. As much as she loved Rita and Arturo, she was too old to need caretakers. She was more than ready to embrace life on her own terms.

She knew Nick was at least a bit of a catalyst in her desire to make some changes. Although she'd been feeling restless, caged in and in need of change for some time, it had taken these two weeks with Nick to solidify her need for action rather than wallowing in dissatisfaction.

She wanted a place of her own, a place where she would be responsible for herself and her own needs, a place that nobody else could claim where she could build a life for herself.

A place where she could cook a meal for a friend, or have a man spend the night. It was time for her to be in charge, to make her own way, make her own decisions and grow.

She tightened her grip on her steering wheel as she thought of Nick. She hadn't been looking for a romantic interest in her life, had never felt the need for a man to make her complete. But she loved spending time with him, talking about everything and nothing with him.

She had never been as comfortable with another person, outside of Jonas. Nick excited her with his heated dark eyes and even hotter touch, but he also put her at ease with his gentle teasing and attentive thoughtfulness.

She was precariously close to being completely in love with him despite the brevity of their relationship so far. She had no idea where their relationship was going, felt no need to worry about it. She simply intended to enjoy each moment as it came.

Slowing her car, she turned into the drive of the cottage that bore Nick's address. It was just as he'd described it, a small bungalow painted white with cheerful yellow trim.

Before she got out of the car, he appeared on the porch. In jeans and a white T-shirt, he looked cool and casual.

He'd told her to dress casually and bring a swimsuit. She wore a pair of red shorts and a red-and-white-striped sleeveless blouse. As she got out of the car she grabbed her purse and her beach bag from the back seat.

"Hi," she said as she approached the porch.

"Hi, yourself. I see you found me all right."

"Your directions were perfect and this place is lovely. It reminds me of an enchanted cottage." She joined him on the porch.

Immediately she recognized an unusual darkness in his eyes, a tension that radiated from him that let her know something was wrong. "Is everything all right?"

"Fine. Come on in." He took her by the elbow and led her through the front door. "I've got the salad made and the charcoal ready for the steaks but thought maybe you'd like to swim a little before we eat."

"Sounds wonderful," she agreed.

He ushered her through the small but comfortable living room and into a bedroom. "You can change into your suit in here. I'll be out on the back deck whenever you're ready."

A moment later, alone in what was obviously the bedroom where he slept while here, Lynn changed into her suit and wondered what was wrong. Even though he'd said everything was fine, she knew something weighed heavily on him.

Just because we've seen each other every night for the past two weeks that doesn't give me the right to pry, she chided herself as she changed into her modest two-piece suit. Two weeks of dating didn't mean he owed her all his thoughts, all his concerns.

As she'd walked through the living room she'd noticed the room contained nothing personal to indicate who lived there. No photos, no knickknacks decorated the room, nothing but an ordinary sofa and chair, small television and coffee table.

Here in the bedroom it was the same. The room contained a double bed, two nightstands and a dresser, but nothing personal. She supposed his apartment at the Heritage Arms was more a reflection of him and had the personal touches that made a place a home.

He hadn't invited her there yet. One day at a time, she reminded herself as she left the bedroom.

As she walked through the kitchen toward the back door, she saw him through the glass windows on the porch. He wore only a pair of black swim trunks, and the sight of his broad tanned chest, slim waist and long muscular legs forced a heat through her entire body. Even though she hadn't been looking for a romantic interest in her life, Nick Barnes made her think of deep kisses and tangled sheets and hot sex.

At that moment he saw her through the glass window and opened the door for her to join him on the deck with its incredible view of beach and ocean.

"Wow, this is great," she said.

He gestured toward the waves. "You ready for a dip?" She nodded. He reached out and grabbed her hand, and together they ran across the expanse of sand and toward the water.

He released his hold on her hand as they both dived into the waves. When she surfaced she saw him just ahead of her, swimming out with strong, sure strokes.

She drew a deep breath and swam toward him. When she caught up with him, she paced him stroke for stroke until he finally surfaced and looked at her in surprise.

"You're a hell of a swimmer," he said.

"What are you doing? Swimming or exorcising demons?" she asked, remembering that he'd said the same thing to her when he'd seen her doing laps in the pool.

"A little of both," he replied, and gestured for them to return to the shore.

Their return was more leisurely as they swam a little and let the waves carry them back in to where they could touch their feet to the ocean floor.

"You want to talk about it?"

He didn't pretend not to know what she meant. "Maybe later," he replied. He swam closer to her. "Right now I just want to play a little."

She squealed as he picked her up and threw her through the air. For the next few minutes they wrestled and dunked each other, playing like children in the invigorating water.

However, Lynn was aware of the fact that there was nothing childlike in the way she felt when her bare legs tangled with his, in how his muscled chest felt beneath her fingertips, in how her breath caught when his hands touched her bare skin.

By the time they left the water, all her senses were heightened to a level she'd never felt before. She wanted him, but he seemed preoccupied as they stood together beneath an outdoor shower to rid themselves of salt residue from the ocean water.

When she'd changed back into her shorts and blouse, she joined him in the kitchen where he was setting the table for their meal.

"What can I do to help?" she asked.

"You can get the salad out of the fridge along with any dressing you want and I'll go turn the steaks. How do you like yours?"

"Medium well."

He nodded and disappeared back outside to the grill. She got out the salad and several bottles of salad dressing, then poured water and ice in glasses and set them on the table.

She went to the door and watched him at the grill. Even though he had been playful in the water, there was a quiet intensity about him she hadn't seen before. She was vaguely surprised to realize the depth of how much she cared that something was obviously bothering him.

He looked up and saw her watching him and motioned for her to come outside. "There's a bottle of wine in the refrigerator. Why don't you pour us each a glass."

"All right." She returned to the kitchen, poured the wine, then once again joined him on the deck.

He took a glass from her, gesturing her toward one of the chairs. "Sit and relax, the steaks will be ready in just a few minutes."

"It's so peaceful out here," she said as she sank into one of the deck chairs. "If I were you, I'd give up my apartment at the Heritage Arms and move in here permanently."

"I need the place close to your godfather's house for business purposes. Nobody knows I have this place, not even your godfather. It's my secret hideaway."

"The enchanted cottage," she repeated, then sipped her wine and digested this information, touched that he'd shared this particular secret with her, even though she sensed he had others.

She thought of all the secrets she possessed. She couldn't really blame him for keeping his when she was keeping so many of her own.

It was after dinner while the two of them were standing at the sink washing their dishes when he finally told her what was bothering him.

"I got a call from my brother this evening. My father wants to see me."

Lynn set her dish towel on the counter and looked at him in surprise. "But that's good news, isn't it? I mean, you told me he'd disowned you and it's been years since you've spoken to him. Maybe he finally wants to fix things, mend fences."

Nick eyed her for a long moment, then placed his palm against her cheek. "You're very sweet." He dropped his hand. "But I doubt very seriously that my father wants to mend fences. He's just not that kind of man."

A deep sadness filled his eyes and it shot straight through to Lynn's heart. She knew the sadness of basically having no family. She couldn't imagine what it would be like to have a family who didn't want you.

This time she placed her palm against Nick's face,

wanting, needing to offer solace. "If he doesn't want to mend fences, then he's nothing but an old fool," she said softly. "Any other man in the world would be proud to have a man like you as a son."

She hadn't intended to kiss him, but she stood so close, and the dark fires in his eyes enticed her forward, to touch his lips with her own. Besides, it wasn't exactly a hardship. She'd learned in the last two weeks that she loved kissing Nick.

He remained perfectly still, his mouth neither accepting nor rejecting hers until she wound her arms around his neck and pressed closer against him. It was only then that he took command of the kiss.

His tongue danced with hers at the same time his arms wrapped around her and he pulled her intimately close against him. Lynn gave herself to the pleasure of his body so tight against hers, his mouth so hot, so hungrily demanding.

She'd never wanted anyone the way she wanted Nick at this moment. As his hold loosened and she sensed he was about to bring the kiss to an end, she leaned even more intimately against him, letting him know she was ready and willing to take it to a new level.

"Lynn," he said as he tore his mouth from hers.

"What?" she asked breathlessly, then trailed kisses along his jawline. She felt the tension in his body and was also aware of his arousal. It reflected the arousal that flowed like hot honey through her veins.

"We should finish the dishes." His voice was husky and thick.

"On the contrary, I think we should finish this." It was the boldest, most forward thing she'd ever said. But for the first time in her life she knew what she wanted and had found the courage to go after it.

Chapter 8

His eyes were darker than she'd ever seen them as he gazed down at her. Hot. Hungry. Yet she also saw a hint of hesitation.

She gave him no opportunity to entertain the latter. She pulled his head down and kissed him once again, her tongue seeking entry into his mouth.

He held himself rigid against her for a long moment, then he groaned as he opened his mouth and returned the kiss. His hands moved up and down her back, beneath her blouse as the fire in the kiss increased.

She could kiss him forever. His kisses were as drugging, as intoxicating as a hundred Alabama Slammers. She loved the warmth of his mouth, the taste of it. She loved the strength of his arms surrounding her, the feel of his body so close to hers. His hands were fevered on her bare skin, and she wanted him touching her everywhere.

She felt not only the beat of his heart against her own, but also the press of his hips into hers and the unmistakable evidence of his desire for her.

He groaned, a deep, husky sound that enflamed her senses further.

At the moment, her gift of heightened senses was truly a treasure. She could not only smell the scent of Nick's cologne but also the fragrance of his laundry detergent and fabric softener in his shirt and the underlying musk of his maleness.

Her fingertips reveled in the feel of his thick, soft hair at the nape of his neck as her body warmed in his embrace.

This time, when the kiss finally ended, it was he who rained kisses down her jaw, into the hollow of her throat. She dropped her head back, allowing him access to the length of her throat. Shivers of pleasure raced up her spine at each touch of his lips against her skin.

She pushed her hips into his, loving the feel of his hardness against her, loving the fact that it was her kisses, her touch that put him in that condition.

Moving her hands down, she felt the taut muscles of his back through his shirt. She wanted to feel his warm skin. She wanted him naked against her.

His hands moved to her sides, slowly caressing upward over her ribs until they rested just beneath her breasts.

Her nipples tingled and hardened as if he'd already touched her there, as if she already felt the heat of his hands on her breasts. Her breath caught in her chest in anticipation, but his hands moved no further.

Instead he dropped his arms to his side and stepped back from her, his gaze not meeting hers. He swiped a hand through his hair, drew a deep breath and finally looked at her.

"Lynn, I want you. Trust me, there's nothing I'd like better than to take you into my bedroom and make love to you until the sun comes up tomorrow morning."

His words, coupled with the desire that flamed in his eyes caused her knees to threaten to buckle. She wanted to tell him that was exactly what she wanted, but her mouth was dry, and before she could speak he continued.

"But we've only been seeing each other for a couple of weeks. I don't want us to rush into this. It's…you're too important to me for that. I don't want to take the chance of any regrets when we do make love."

Disappointment swept through her, but it was a disappointment tempered by the fact that he obviously had her best interest at heart. It *had* only been a couple of weeks, even though it felt much longer. Even though she'd never felt this way about any man before, that didn't mean it wasn't wise to go slowly.

"Then I guess we'd better finish the dishes," she said, her voice breathy and slightly unsteady.

"I guess we'd better," he agreed.

They finished the dishes, then carried wine out to the patio and sat to watch the waves rushing to shore as the last of daylight slipped away.

"This is my favorite time of day," she said as she watched the splash of the sun's last light gleaming on the water.

"I'm a dawn kind of person myself," he replied. "Especially when I'm here at the cottage and can watch the sun come up."

As they talked, Lynn was aware of the simmering tension between them, a tension she knew was blatantly sexual.

But certainly her attraction to Nick wasn't just sexual in nature. There seemed to be a chemistry at work between them, one that went beyond mere physical attraction. She'd never felt this way about another person before in her life.

Although she felt wonderfully at ease with him, she

also felt a spark of electricity, the promise of endless possibilities whenever she was with him.

"To me, dawn is always about the possibilities the day might hold, and dusk is always about reflections of what the day did hold," she said.

He smiled, his features barely discernible in the growing darkness of night. "And what are you reflecting about at this moment?"

"About what a lovely evening I've had." Her cheeks warmed slightly, and she smiled shyly. "And about how much I enjoy spending time with you."

"I feel the same way," he said after a moment's hesitation. "You're easy to be with, Lynn. You don't seem like most twenty-two-year-olds."

"What does that mean?" she asked, unsure whether to be offended or pleased.

He looked out at the water and sighed thoughtfully. "I don't know, you just seem older, more mature and more sure of yourself."

She laughed. "Get me in a room with more than three people in it and you'll see just how unsure I can be of myself."

"That has nothing to do with maturity," he countered. "Lots of people are shy. From what I know, you just haven't had a chance to practice the skills of socializing with a lot of people, apart from your friends at school."

"That's definitely true." It was her turn to stare out

at the water, where the sun had gone away and moonlight cast a faint silvery illumination onto the tips of the waves. "But you're right, I don't think I'm like other women my age. My peers were always my godfather and his friends. I never really had friends my own age until the last couple of years."

"All I know is that you seem older, more settled than most young women I've known."

She looked at him once again. "I'm going to take that as a compliment."

He laughed. "Good, because I meant it as one."

He'd told her earlier in the evening that he was on security duty that night at midnight, so when eleven arrived, she stood to prepare to leave.

"I'll follow you to the house," he said, also rising from the deck chair.

"Do you often work the overnight hours?" she asked as they walked through the house toward the front door.

"Not often, but occasionally. One of my men called in sick this afternoon so I'm working for him tonight." His hand in the small of her back as he led her out the door was a reminder of what they had almost shared, what they would have shared had he not stopped it.

He opened her car door, then leaned forward and captured her lips with a gentle kiss that was every bit as seductive as the hotter, deeper kisses they had shared earlier.

"I won't be able to see you tomorrow night," he said when the kiss ended. "I have that reunion with my family."

"I hope it goes well for you."

He smiled. "I'm not expecting any miracles." His smile faded and instead his gaze on her was darkly serious. "Sometimes you just have to face the fact that the people who raise you, the people who are supposed to love and guide you, the people who are supposed to teach you right from wrong and good from bad, don't always have your best interests at heart. Not everyone who has children deserves them."

Confusion swept through her. She had the feeling he wasn't just talking about his own situation, but somehow was trying to say something to her personally.

However, there was no way she could compare Nick's family to her godfather. Jonas had taken care of her, supported her and loved her every day that she had been in his life.

"You'll call me tomorrow night…if you need to talk?" she asked.

He smiled and reached out to brush a strand of her hair away from her cheek. "I'll call you even if I don't need to talk." He leaned forward and gave her a chaste kiss on the forehead. "Drive safely going home. I'll be right behind you."

As she got into her car, she was aware of him getting into his behind her. Within minutes she was back on the highway heading home, her thoughts filled with the evening she had just shared with Nick.

The fact that he'd halted any lovemaking, proclaiming that he wanted to wait to make sure it was right for both of them only made her want him more. How many men would have done what he'd done? Not many, she thought.

Lynn had no idea if Nick was the man who would be in her life forever. She had no idea if they had a future of endless nights together or only a few. That didn't matter. She knew with certainty that she wanted to make love to him, that she wanted to experience for the first time total intimacy with him. Beyond that, she didn't know what the future held for the two of them.

When she reached the house, she zoomed through the opened gates and Nick followed her in. As she pulled up and parked, he waved and drove around the back of the house where the security shed was located.

She got out of her car and was almost to the porch when she felt the hair at the nape of her neck raise in a subliminal warning. She froze as she had the distinct impression that she was being watched.

Narrowing her gaze, she looked all around, seeking a reason for her uneasy feeling. But she saw nothing out of the ordinary. Here, behind the gates of her home, should be the safest place in the world. The security was top-notch, and surely there was no way anyone who shouldn't be on the property would be on the property.

Maybe she was still suffering some sort of paranoid reaction to her encounter with the FBI the other night. Even though she still felt as if somebody…or something was out there in the dark, watching her, she turned and went into the house.

Inside she was greeted by the relative silence of a house at rest. The whoosh of the air conditioner cooling the air, the tick of the antique clock on the mantel in the living room and the creak of the stairs leading up to her room welcomed her with familiarity, and she felt herself once again relaxing.

When she reached her room, she went into the bathroom and removed her makeup, washed her face and brushed her teeth, then pulled on the short pink silk nightgown she usually wore to bed.

She had just gotten into bed when she heard the faint, but unmistakable sound of glass breaking. She sat up, heart pounding. The sound had come from someplace downstairs.

She flew from the bed and took the stairs two at a time. She couldn't be certain, but she thought the sound had come from the back of the house, in the living room area.

As she entered the living room she turned on the light switch and saw movement at the French doors that led out to the patio. The pane of glass next to the door lock was broken out. Apparently that's what she'd heard shattering.

She didn't hesitate, but ran to the doors, unlocked them and threw them open. In the shadows of the night she saw a figure racing away. Without conscious thought, she took off after the dark figure.

She ran as fast as she could, surprised that she gained nothing on the intruder, who flew like the wind. When she was halfway to the high wall that surrounded the perimeter of the compound, bright floodlights lit the area enough for her to see the figure leap to the top of the wall then disappear over it.

She slowed, her breath coming in labored gasps as she realized by the time she reached the wall, the intruder would be long gone.

"Lynn!"

She whirled around to see Nick running toward her. "Somebody tried to break into the house," she gasped as she tried to catch her breath.

He touched her arm, his features as hard and set as she'd ever seen them. "Are you all right?"

She nodded. "Whoever it was is gone." She pointed toward the wall. "He went over the top." She drew several more deep breaths, then continued. "I've never seen anyone so fast. It was inhuman!"

Nick stared at her for a long moment, but before he could say anything else to her, several other security guards came running toward them.

His gaze raked the length of her and he tightened his grip on her arm. "Scan the perimeter then go back to your posts," he yelled to the approaching men, then looked at her once again. "Let's get you inside."

It wasn't until that moment that she realized how skimpily she was dressed. The silk nightgown clung to her, making her look almost naked with her nipples hardened by the night air and her exertions.

She was grateful he'd kept the other men away. She didn't mind Nick seeing her in this condition, but she certainly didn't want any of the other men to see her like this.

Together they walked back to the house. "What I'd like to know is how the intruder got past the security cameras," he said more to himself than to her.

Lynn said nothing. Her mind whirled with troubling thoughts. At least she knew now she hadn't been paranoid. She'd sensed somebody watching her and somebody *had* been out there. But who? And why would they want to get into the house?

And who could run so fast…as fast as she could?

When they reached the French doors Lynn excused herself to run upstairs and get a robe as Nick studied the broken glass.

Minutes later when she returned, he'd positioned a piece of wood over the broken pane of glass and stood at the edge of the patio, staring out into the darkness. "I need to check the security tapes, although

I was sitting at the desk watching the cameras and didn't see anyone come or go over the wall."

"I'd like to go with you," she replied. She wanted to know how somebody had managed to slip past security. She needed to see if the cameras had caught a picture of who had been on the property.

She followed him around the side of the house and to the shed that served as security headquarters. Lynn had never been in the shed before and was astonished by the elaborate bank of monitors that lined one wall.

"The cameras monitor the front gate and all along the perimeter of the compound," he said. "There are a total of twenty cameras." He pointed to one of the monitors. "That's the one that should have shown me our intruder going over the wall to escape." He pushed several buttons on a large console.

"I know it sounds crazy, but when I got out of my car and was walking to the front door, I sensed somebody nearby," she said.

He frowned thoughtfully and sat in the chair in front of the control panel. "We got here around eleven-thirty, and if you sensed somebody hanging around, that means whoever it was came over the wall sometime before eleven-thirty."

The picture on the monitor began to rewind, small numbers in the corner providing a time stamp. "Is everything recorded?" she asked, wondering how many times they had recorded her leaving the premises for one of her middle-of-the-night retrievals.

"Yeah, everything is on a seventy-two-hour loop, so the recorded images are kept for three days, then the tape is recorded over." He stopped the tape. The time stamp in the corner read 10:00 p.m.

"Can you tell by this picture where exactly he went over the wall?" he asked.

She frowned and studied the frozen picture intently. "There," she said and pointed. "It was just to the right of that tree."

Nick fast-forwarded the picture and they both watched the screen. Lynn gasped as the dark figure appeared and seemed to fly over the wall.

Nick stopped the tape, rewound it and played it again. He played it a total of three times, then stopped the tape and turned to Lynn. "I've never seen anyone move that fast in my life. What do you think—male or female?"

"Hard to say. With the mask and all it could be either." Whoever it was had been wearing black clothing, and with the darkness of night it was hard to discern a distinctive body shape.

"We see how he got out, but we don't see how he got in." Once again Nick rewound the tape and they watched it in fast motion, beginning at eight in the evening. Nothing. Nick checked all the camera angles, but they couldn't find out how the intruder had entered the premises.

A muscle ticked in Nick's jaw. "There must be a flaw in the security. And the only way an outsider could know about a flaw is if they studied the entire system or somebody from the security team identified the flaw and told them. Both situations concern me."

What concerned Lynn was the speed with which the figure had shot across the lawn. Lynn had never met another person in her life that she couldn't out-run…until now.

"So what happens now?" she asked.

He leaned back in his chair, a frown furrowing his forehead. "I need to write a report and talk to Jonas and see what he wants to do."

"When I spoke to him this morning, he said he wouldn't be contacting me for the next few days and I wouldn't be able to get in touch with him."

"Did he say when he'd be back here?"

She nodded. "He said he'd be back sometime on Monday."

"Then I guess I'll talk to him when he returns." He swiped a hand through his thick, dark hair. "In the meantime, I'll add a couple of extra guards to walk the perimeter during the nighttime hours."

His features were taut as his gaze once again raked over the length of her. "You were foolish to chase after him." There was anger in his gaze coupled with the heat of a deeper emotion.

"I didn't think. I just reacted. I had just gotten into bed when I heard the sound of breaking glass." Every inch of bared skin prickled beneath the heat of his gaze.

"I know there's a panic room in the house. You should have immediately locked yourself inside and called for security."

Lynn thought of the small room that was hidden inside Jonas's bedroom closet. The bulletproof, fireproof panic room was another of Jonas's whims.

She wasn't going to argue with Nick, but there was no way she'd lock herself into that tiny room and wait for help to reach her. She suffered from just enough claustrophobia that the very idea caused her skin to crawl.

She would much prefer to depend on her physical skills and face head-on whatever danger might be present, instead of hiding in what felt far too much like a small, steel-enclosed coffin.

Nick stood and held out a hand toward her. "Come on, I'll walk you back to the house. There's nothing more that can be done tonight."

She allowed him to pull her up from her chair, and together they left the shed and walked to the back of the house. She saw several guards in the distance, walking the perimeter of the back wall.

When they reached the back door he turned to face her, his gaze solemn. He reached out and grabbed the ends of the robe belt and pulled them to tighten the robe around her. "Promise me you won't ever do anything so foolish again," he said. "I don't want anything bad to happen to you."

Heat blossomed in the pit of her stomach, created both by his words and by his close proximity. "I promise."

He used the ends of her belt to draw her closer until her lips were mere inches from his. "I don't know what I'd do if anything happened to you." He gave her no opportunity to reply, but instead took her mouth with his in a kiss that stole her breath away.

When the kiss finally ended, she wanted nothing more than to invite him inside with her, take him to her room and make love with him beneath the canopy above her bed.

He seemed to sense her thoughts, her desire, and he released the ends of her belt and stepped back from her. "Go to bed, Lynn. It's late and I've got to get back to the security shed."

"I'll sleep better knowing you're there."

He smiled, touched her cheek with the back of his hand, then turned and walked away. Lynn waited until he was out of sight, then she went inside and carefully locked the door behind her.

Even the warm glow of Nick couldn't banish the troubling thoughts that stirred in her head as she once again went up the stairs to her bedroom.

Who had been on the property? Who had tried to break into the house? Somehow she couldn't believe it was an ordinary thief. No common thief would attempt a robbery at a place that boasted camera surveillance and guards.

No ordinary person could run like that. No ordinary person could leap a high wall like the intruder had done.

There was only one person Lynn knew who was capable of such things, and that was her. Lynn remembered the fantasies she used to entertain about having a sibling. She knew she didn't—Jonas surely would have known and told her—but perhaps it was possible she had other family out there. It had been a long time since she'd read the news reports about her parents. Perhaps it was time to look at them again.

Nick sat in front of the bank of monitors staring blankly at first one, then another. The attempted break-in had him disturbed on two levels. First, he couldn't believe that somebody had managed to breach the security, had figured out where one of the blind spots was and had exploited it.

More important, he was disturbed by what Lynn had said when he'd caught up with her in the backyard. Superhuman speed and agility and strength to match, those were the same qualities used to describe the superthief who had been plaguing the department for the past two years.

Nick had always believed Jonas was tied to those robberies. Was it possible that the thief had come here tonight to check in with his boss, not knowing that the boss was out of the country? If that was the case, Lynn fell off his list of suspects. Still he'd stick to the decision he'd made to tail her on her nightly drives for a while. Just to cover all bases.

He raked a hand down his face and straightened his back, trying to ease some of the tension that had been with him all evening.

The phone call from his brother had started the first stir of stress. The idea of seeing his father had created a ball of tension in his chest, and being with Lynn, fighting his intense desire for her, had merely served to heighten it.

He thought of those moments earlier in the evening, when her mouth had been so hot against his, when she'd pressed her body so close that he could feel every curve beneath her clothing.

She'd wanted him to take her to bed, to make love to her, and he'd wanted it more than he could remember wanting a woman before in his life.

The most difficult thing he'd ever done was to deny his own desire and call a halt to those kisses.

As if that hadn't been difficult enough, seeing her in that skimpy, sexy nightgown—her nipples thrusting out as if to taunt him and her breasts heaving from her exertion—had nearly undone him.

He'd wanted to take her in his arms and pull her down in the sweet lush grass and make her moan as she'd never moaned before. He'd wanted to lose himself in the pleasure of making love to her.

Dammit.

Business and pleasure were mingling together in a dangerous way. Even though his instinct was to protect Lynn, he had to focus on getting the information he needed from her.

He couldn't afford to get soft. Too much time and too much money had already been spent in an effort to bring down Jonas White.

No matter how much he wanted to spare Lynn from the truth about her godfather, tomorrow he was going to step up his campaign with her. He wanted access to financial records, and he needed to see who, exactly, Jonas kept on his payroll.

He had a feeling that somewhere in those records he would find the identity of the superthief and the information to bring Jonas down. He just hoped Lynn didn't get crushed in the process.

Chapter 9

The next morning Lynn went to class unusually early. She wanted some extra time alone in the computer lab. Although the computer search she intended to conduct could have been done at home on her godfather's computer, she preferred doing it in the neutral territory of a classroom.

Before heading for the lab, she went to the student union, wanting to fortify herself with an extra cup of coffee before getting down to work.

Even though it was early, the student union was hopping with people, most utilizing the coffeemaker and the vending machine that offered snack substitutes for breakfast.

She got her coffee, then with surprise spied Sonya looking half-asleep and more than a bit grumpy, seated at a table alone. She made her way to the table.

"What on earth are you doing here so early?" she asked her friend.

Sonya wrinkled her nose in disgust. "In half an hour a bunch of us are supposed to start painting sets for the play."

Lynn sank down in the chair next to her friend. "Painting sets? But I thought you were the leading lady."

Sonya snorted indelicately. "Yeah, right. Leading lady, set painter, prop getter, costume seamstress. I can't wait until I work on a production that has a bigger budget than a buck eighty-five."

Lynn laughed. "Just think of everything you're learning."

"What I'd like to learn is what it's like to have a personal assistant and make more money than Oprah. I'd like to learn what it's like to get dressed in Dior or Chanel for the Oscars and be nominated for three different awards."

"Give it time, Sonya. If you want it badly enough it will eventually happen for you."

"I suppose. What are you doing here so early?" Sonya grabbed her coffee cup and took a deep drink.

"I wanted to get in some extra time in the computer lab."

Again Sonya wrinkled her nose. "Sounds perfectly

boring. So tell me what's been going on with you. You've been pretty scarce since that night at Sensations. And what about that hunk who took you home from there?"

"You mean Nick?" Despite her best efforts, Lynn felt the blush she knew reddened her cheeks. "I told you that night that he works security for Jonas."

"Right. So, where have you been keeping yourself the last couple of weeks? You haven't even made it to the Cloister for coffee lately." Sonya raised one of her perfectly plucked eyebrows. "It's been my experience that when a woman stops meeting with her friends, there's a male somewhere in the picture. So tell me, where have you been and with whom?"

Lynn's blush grew hotter. It was true, she hadn't spent much time with her friends in the past couple of weeks. After her classes she'd hurried home each afternoon to see Nick. "I've been here and there."

Sonya eyed her narrowly. "It's a guy, isn't it? I can tell. You've got that look about you. It's the security guy, isn't it." She smiled like the proverbial Cheshire cat. "There's more going on between you two than just the fact that he works for your godfather."

The desire to tell somebody how she felt about Nick was suddenly overwhelming. She reached out and grabbed Sonya's hand. "Yes, there's more to it than that. We've been seeing each other every night for the past two weeks. Oh, Sonya, I've never felt this way about anyone before. He excites me, yet puts me at ease at the same time."

She paused, aware that she hadn't even begun to explain how she felt whenever she was with Nick. No words could adequately describe what she felt.

"Oh, girl, you got it bad. I see it in your eyes."

Lynn laughed once again. "I've got it so bad it feels good."

Sonya squeezed her hand, her features unusually somber. "Go slow, Lynnie. If this Nick is really special, then take it slow and savor every moment."

"I am…I mean, we are."

"Good." Sonya released her hand. "And of course it goes without saying that you need to remember that a man is a luxury, not a necessity for women in our generation."

"Don't worry, I don't need a man to complete me," Lynn said dryly. "But I sure enjoy spending time with him."

"From what I remember of him, the man isn't exactly hard to look at."

"No, he isn't, and what's even better, he's a good guy."

"Then, honey, hang on to him. They don't always come as a complete package." Sonya checked her watch, then jumped up. "I've gotta split. We were told if we arrived late this morning then we'd be spending our Friday night painting sets. Like I want to do

that. Call me," she said over her shoulder as she hurried away.

Lynn remained at the table and finished her coffee,
her thoughts on Nick and what Sonya had said about
women of their generation.

Certainly Lynn wasn't one of those women who
desperately needed a man in her life, who defined
who she was by what a man thought of her. She was
just beginning the process of defining herself.

Nor was she in a hurry for marriage. Someday
she'd like to bind her life to a man's, but certainly not
anytime soon. That didn't mean she didn't want a real
relationship based on not only sexual desire but emotional intimacy, as well.

She dumped her empty foam coffee cup in the
trash, then headed for the computer lab. As she took
a seat at one of the computers, she wasn't alone in the
room. Several other students were already working.
She waved to a guy she knew, then settled in and pow-
ered up the machine.

It was funny, for the past few weeks since spending time with Nick, she'd spent less time chatting on
her computer. It was so much more wonderful having
a real relationship instead of one built on technology.

She shoved thoughts of Nick away and focused on
the reason she'd come to the lab in the first place.

It had been years ago, when she'd been thirteen,
that Jonas had first shown her the news accounts of

her parents' deaths. At that time Lynn had been hungry for any detail of their lives and deaths.

Jonas had saved clippings and photos to answer her questions about where and whom she had come from. He'd also shown her a bank book that contained the information about the trust fund her parents had left behind for her. When she got older, the realization had sunk in that she was a wealthy woman in her own right.

Seeing the figure run across the grounds with a speed and agility to match her own had ignited questions. What had the person wanted? Was there something she didn't know about herself?

She knew the computers here at the college were linked to all kinds of news services and also tied into the college library system of newspapers from the last thirty years or so. She should have no problem pulling up those old news stories that Jonas had shown her so many years ago.

It took her only minutes to pull up the link to the *Miami Herald*. In the search box she put her parents' names, Malcolm and Anne Winters, then she added the words, yacht…drowning and storm.

The results she got were overwhelming, and she realized quickly she had to narrow down the search. It had been foolish for her to put the words drowning and storm in a search of a Miami newspaper. Every year there were dozens of storms and drownings in the area.

Once again she typed into the search box, this time listing only her parents' names. It took only seconds for her to get the dialogue box NO MATCHES FOUND.

She frowned and tapped her index finger against the mouse. She had no idea how sensitive the search function might be for old newspapers.

Her parents had died when she was five months old. She'd been born in December. That meant her parents had to have died in the month of April. She would have to read the papers for that month and see if she could find any report of the accident and storm that had claimed their lives.

There was no way she was going to make her classes today. This was far more important than any-thing she could learn from a teacher. She intended to sit here until she got some information.

Once again she thought of the person she'd seen running across the backyard the night before. She had no idea if the person had been male or female. All she knew was that the person had run like the wind…run like her.

Jonas had always told her she was an anomaly, that her unusual speed and agility, her heightened senses had been some sort of genetic gift. If that was true, then how was it possible that there might be somebody else like her?

Hours later she leaned back in the chair and moved

her shoulders up and down in an attempt to alleviate some of the exhaustion that weighed her down.

Nothing.

She'd found nothing about the boating accident that had taken her parents away from her. She'd gone through every newspaper for the month of April. There had been stories about murders and robberies, fires and even a shark attack or two, but nothing about a millionaire and his wife dying in a storm.

But she'd seen the clippings. So, why hadn't she been able to find them?

As she drove home, she once again thought of the person who had tried to get into the house the night before. And thinking back, she remembered several times when she'd had the feeling she was being watched, that somebody was nearby.

Was it possible the FBI were watching her? That somehow they'd tied her to the thefts of precious artifacts? Was it possible Jonas's contact hadn't straightened things out with that agency after all?

She shook her head. That didn't make sense. She could understand the FBI watching her, watching the house but why would any of them try to break in? If they wanted in, if they wanted her, they'd get a warrant and show up at the front door. She wouldn't have been left to chase after the person and she would have left the house in handcuffs.

Confusion stayed with her when she got back

home. She was vaguely disappointed that Nick wasn't waiting for her when she pulled through the gates. She'd gotten accustomed to him meeting her each day after her classes. But he'd worked all night and had probably gone home to get some sleep before meeting with his family this evening.

She hoped the meeting went well. It would be nice if his family made peace with him and erased some of the dark shadows she occasionally saw flit across his eyes. She knew that hunger for family and she hoped Nick's problems with his were resolved.

A wonderful fragrance of apples and cinnamon wafted in the air when she entered the house. Lynn followed the scent into the kitchen where Rita sat at the table with a cup of coffee in front of her.

"Apple pie?" Lynn asked.

"Dumplings." Rita looked over at the clock on the oven. "You're later than usual. Did you have coffee with your friends?"

Lynn slid into the chair opposite the housekeeper. "No, I didn't even go to classes today."

Rita looked at her in surprise. "Is everything all right?"

Her first instinct was to reassure the plump Cuban woman that everything was fine. But it wasn't fine, and Lynn wasn't going to pretend it was. She released a deep sigh. "No, everything isn't all right. I'm confused, Rita."

"Confused about what?"

"My parents died in a boating accident in a storm when I was five months old." Rita nodded and Lynn continued. "But I just spent the morning going through all the local and national newspapers for the month and that whole year, and I can't find any record of such an accident."

Rita frowned. "I'm sure there must be a logical explanation for that. You know Mr. Jonas has always said your parents were eccentric. Maybe the story was intentionally kept out of the papers for some reason or another."

Lynn shook her head. "No, that's not right, because a long time ago Jonas showed me news clippings about the accident. Not only were there reports about their accident, but there were also several about my father's philanthropic work with charitable foundations."

Rita shrugged. "I don't know anything about clippings." Her dark eyes filled with concern. "What's wrong, Lynn? Why are you looking for reports of tragedy?"

She thought carefully before answering. Why was it suddenly so important that she know more? Because she'd seen somebody possibly as skilled as her. Because the image of that person running and leaping had put questions into her head. "I'm curious. It's been a long time since I read about my parents. I guess I'm hungry to know more about them."

"You're just feeling lonely. Things will be better when Mr. Jonas returns. He'll have the answers you need."

"I'm sure you're right," Lynn replied, then excused herself.

A few minutes later she called her uncle from her room, unsurprised when the call went directly to his voice mail. He'd said he wouldn't be communicating until he returned home on Monday.

He must be in the middle of some intense negotiations, probably on a defense contract. She wished he were here to answer her questions. She wished she'd asked more questions in the past.

She walked over to her window and stared outside. From this vantage point she could see the perimeter wall in the distance and her gaze went directly to the place where she'd seen the figure disappear over the wall the night before. She tapped a finger against the glass, then sighed and turned away.

She was going after the urn and vase tonight. She was banking on the fact that nobody would be prepared for lightning to strike twice in the same place. The FBI had thwarted her two weeks ago at the Markham Convention Center. She was gambling that they would never think she'd attempt to get into the same place so soon after the failed attempt.

She had no intention of changing her routine. She knew the security cameras would capture her leaving, but tonight would be no different from any other night. There was no way she could be tied to the robberies. She'd long ago established a pattern that would make it difficult for anyone to prove what she did when she left the house each night.

She spent most of the afternoon going over her plans again and again. She checked and rechecked the floor plans for the convention center, making sure there was nothing she'd missed in her initial research.

Dinner was a quiet affair with Rita and Arturo in the kitchen. Arturo spent the meal entertaining her with stories about his childhood in Cuba and she wondered if Rita had told her husband that Lynn was depressed. Love for the couple filled her heart.

When dinner was finished she returned to her room. At six-thirty her phone rang. She half hoped it was Jonas, but was pleasantly surprised to hear Nick's voice.

"Hi…where are you?" she asked.

"At the enchanted cottage. I needed a little quiet time before heading into the lion's den."

"Oh, Nick. I hope things go well for you. It would be wonderful if you could have some sort of relationship with your family again."

"We'll see how things go," he replied. It was obvious from his tone of voice that he had no expectations about his night to come.

"I spent the day trying to find information about my parents," she confessed.

"Really? What did you find out?"

"Nothing. Absolutely nothing." She ran a hand over the brocade material of her bedspread, her fingers tracing the lines of one of the lavender flowers that decorated the spread.

"Where did you look?"

She told him about the unsuccessful newspaper search. "I even did a Web search and came up with nothing. Jonas showed me news clippings about them, and the accident years ago, but I couldn't find any record of them."

"Have you asked Jonas about it?"

She sighed. "I haven't had a chance. He's still not answering his phone. I'm going to talk to him about them as soon as he gets back home."

"What are your plans for this evening?" he asked.

"I'm going to study for a test I have next week, then go to bed early." She hated to lie to him, but the last thing she wanted was to bring trouble to his door if trouble should come. Better he not know anything about the work she did for Jonas and the government. Eventually, if their relationship continued, then she'd share all of her secrets with him.

"Lynn, I've been thinking about that intruder last night."

"What about it?"

"I can't help but think that it might have been an inside job, and I have a favor to ask of you."

"What?"

"You mentioned before that you keep the books for Jonas. Does that mean you also take care of his payroll?"

"Yes, I do. Why?"

"I'd like a copy of everyone who is on the payroll. I'd like to do some background checks and see if we can find out if somebody who works here was the person who tried to break in."

Lynn sat up on the bed. "But why would somebody who works for us try to break into the house?"

"For starters, if somebody is having financial problems, it's possible they or someone connected to them might have taken a chance."

"All right. I guess I could get you a list of the people who work for Uncle Jonas," she said.

"I have one more favor," he said. "Could we keep this just between you and me? I hate to ask you to keep secrets, but I'd prefer Jonas doesn't know about it until I've checked everyone out."

He wasn't asking her to lie, he was simply asking her to keep silent until he could sort things out. "I don't have a problem with that. I'll have the list for you first thing in the morning."

"Great. If I can find the culprit before Jonas gets home, then I'll feel better about the security breach."

She hadn't realized until this moment just how personally he was taking the security problem. "It's no problem, Nick." She looked at her wristwatch. "And shouldn't you be leaving? You don't want to be late for the meeting with your family."

"Yeah, you're right. Guess it's time for me to head out of here. How about we go back to Smokey's tomorrow night?" His voice deepened. "I'm in the mood to dance with you again."

Pleasure swept through her. "Sounds wonderful. Just let me know when and I'll be ready."

"I'll call you tomorrow to set up a time."

"Nick, good luck tonight."

"Thanks, I'll call you tomorrow." With these words he clicked off.

She left her bedroom and went downstairs to the study, where Jonas's computer sat, ready for use. This was the computer she often worked on when she was doing work for her godfather.

She'd never wandered through the files before. Usually she pulled up the financial program she used and did whatever needed to be done. This time she pulled up a directory and studied the files contained on the hard drive.

Maybe there was something about her parents in a file, some information that would tell her more about them, about what kind of people they had been.

She opened dozens of files but found nothing of interest. She finally pulled up the payroll records and printed them to give to Nick. Then she shut off the computer and carried the papers upstairs with her.

The rest of the evening stretched out before her. It would be hours before she would be able to leave to get the urn that Jonas had indicated he wanted.

Nothing had been as hurtful to her as Jonas questioning her ability to continue to help him in this work. She had to get the urn to reaffirm his belief in her, and she needed to get the urn to reaffirm her belief in herself and her ability to do the work that Jonas loved.

It was midnight when she left the house. Clad in jeans and a T-shirt, she walked with the nonchalance of a woman with nothing to hide, as if this night was like a hundred other nights.

The trunk of her car contained all that she would need: dark clothing, a stocking cap and the tools of the trade all neatly packed in an oversize book bag.

She got into her car and punched the remote button to open the gates at the end of the driveway. As she left the house behind, she focused on the next step. About three miles down the road was a liquor store that had gone out of business. The alley behind the place was a perfect place for her to change clothes and prepare for the job ahead.

Within minutes she was back in the car clad in black jeans and a long-sleeved black T-shirt. As she drove, she drew deep breaths, centering herself for the task ahead, hoping she was right that nobody would suspect the convention center would be hit again so soon after the last failed robbery.

She was also praying that Jonas's contact hadn't lied to him and the situation with the FBI had been resolved.

She parked her car in front of a house in a residential neighborhood three blocks away from the convention center. After the job was done, she'd drive for another hour or so, putting additional miles on the car so time and distance couldn't be matched up.

She wasn't going in the same way she had last week. She'd found another air vent that led to what appeared to be a small janitorial closet.

It would be a little trickier, as this particular vent was on the side of the building rather than in the back. She'd have to keep an eye out for security guards.

When she reached the side of the convention center, she crouched in the shadows of a large bush and eyed the scene before her. Thankfully there was little light on this side of the building, just enough for her to see the vent she intended to use to get inside.

She pulled on gloves, then exchanged the ball cap for the stocking cap to completely hide her hair. She cocked her head and listened, ignoring the audible beat of her own heart to focus on the noise surrounding her.

She heard the scrape of boots against the concrete walk out front, heard the strike of a match and the intake of breath as one of the guards lit a cigarette.

There seemed to be only one guard on duty, and

while he smoked his cigarette Lynn removed the cover of the vent and slithered through. Once inside she turned back to the vent cover and balanced it so it looked as if it hadn't been removed, then she clicked on her penlight to orient herself.

Just as she'd hoped, she found herself in a small room used to store janitorial supplies. The air in the room was thick with the scent of astringent ammonia, bathroom deodorizer and floor wax.

The penlight showed metal shelving units of supplies, not only the cleaning items, but also rolls of toilet tissue and paper towels.

She moved to the doorway that would lead her out of the supply closet and pressed her ear against the door. She heard absolutely nothing to indicate any human presence on the other side of the door.

She shut off her penlight, twisted the doorknob and eased the door open, grateful there was no squeak or groan. Once again she stood perfectly still and listened. Again she heard nothing to cause her alarm.

The hallway outside the closet was dark, but she knew from studying the floor plans that if she followed it to the right it would lead her into the main artery that ran between the various exhibit rooms.

Using a hand to anchor herself against one wall, she moved silently, slipping over, under and around the laser alarms, eager to get the job done and get back home. For the first time since she'd begun this work for Jonas, it didn't feel quite right. Her instincts were all screaming that something was off.

She reached the end of the hallway and paused, her senses all alive. So far so good. She hadn't really expected trouble, and so far she hadn't found any.

Her heartbeat accelerated when she reached the lobby area that she would have to cross to get to the room where the Treasure of the Nile exhibit was being held. It was in this same area she had nearly been caught a week before.

Tonight faint moonlight drifted in through the bank of windows, illuminating just enough of the area for her to see there seemed to be nothing amiss.

She took a step out of the dark hallway, then another and another. Suddenly every light in the place flashed on, momentarily blinding her. Panic clawed up her throat.

"Freeze," several voices shouted. One came from in front of her, another from behind her, letting her know that this time there was no escape.

Chapter 10

"Get those hands up where we can see them," one of the men yelled. "Simms, call headquarters and tell them we have the perp in custody."

Lynn thought of fighting, of using her skills to try to escape. But rational thought won over emotional impulse. There were too many of them and they had guns. She slowly raised her hands above her head as her vision adjusted to the bright overhead lights.

Six men surrounded her. They all wore black T-shirts with the yellow FBI acronym emblazoned across their chests and backs. She should have heard them, their breathing, but she'd been too focused on the alarm sensors, on getting in and out.

"There's been a mistake," Lynn began, her heart knocking almost painfully against her ribs.

"Yeah, your mistake." A tall blond-haired man with cold blue eyes approached her. "You got any ID on you? Any weapons?"

"No…neither," she replied. To her horror he patted her down. It was both intrusive and humiliating. He checked her pockets, then took her backpack off her back.

"We've been waiting for you, sweetheart," the blonde said. "We've been hoping you'd come back to see us after the last little fiasco."

"How did you know I'd come back?" she asked, curious as to how they'd guessed this would be a target and not someplace else.

"We weren't sure. We've got teams set up all over Miami in museums and galleries just hoping you'd show." Lynn slowly digested this information. "What's your name?" he asked when he'd finished frisking her.

She hesitated a moment, then decided there was no reason not to cooperate with them to the fullest. Surely when they got to the station or wherever they would be taking her, the whole thing would be straightened out and she'd be released immediately.

"Lynnette White."

"Ms. White, put your hands behind your back. You're under arrest for attempted robbery and suspicion of several other robberies."

The snap of the handcuffs around her wrists sounded like gunfire in her ear. The cuffs were cold and tight. As the agent began to lead her toward the entrance of the convention center, he read her her rights.

This will all be straightened out soon, she told herself as the officer's words rang in her ears. There was no point in trying to explain things to these men. She needed to talk to somebody in charge.

A phone call from Jonas or the contact he had with the government would surely effect her immediate release. All she needed to do was be patient and stay calm. However, it was difficult to stay calm with her hands cuffed behind her. It seemed to take forever before she was finally led toward the entrance of the convention center.

The thick night air wrapped around her as she was led to the door of the building. They had just stepped out when a car screeched to a halt in front of the building. She stared at the car…a familiar car.

For a moment her mind refused to make any sense of it. It looked like Nick's car, but that didn't make any sense at all. What would he be doing here?

Her heart leaped as a thought occurred to her. Maybe he was here to help her. Maybe Uncle Jonas had sent him. But even as she thought it, she knew it was impossible. How could he be here to help her? How could he or her Uncle Jonas know she was in trouble?

She stared in confusion as he stepped out of the car.

"Agent Barnes," the officer behind her yelled. "We got the perp."

Agent Barnes? For a moment her mind simply refused to understand. Agent Barnes? Nick was Agent Barnes? But he worked for Jonas. He was head of security.

His gaze met hers, and in his eyes she knew the truth. He was an FBI agent. Numbness swept through her as their gazes remained locked for a long moment. With a gasp, she tore her gaze from his.

Moments later as she sat in the back of a car driving her to wherever they intended to take her, her mind tried to wrap around what she had just learned.

Agent Barnes. FBI Agent Nick Barnes. When their gazes had met for that single moment, she'd seen the shock in his gaze, but no amount of shock he felt in seeing her could compare to what she felt at seeing him, at learning who he was.

She closed her eyes and leaned back, instantly feeling the painful pinch of the cuffs biting into her wrists. She welcomed the physical pain that momentarily obscured anything else she might feel. Tears burned at her eyes, but she focused only on the pain at her wrists.

Soon enough the cuffs would be removed, the numbness of shock would wear off and she'd have to face emotions she didn't want to feel.

The blessed numbness remained with her as she was taken into the local precinct. She was finger-printed and her mug shot taken, then finally she was led into a small interrogation room.

The room was like something from a movie, containing a table and two chairs and nothing else that could be used as a weapon against an officer or herself. A long mirror stretched across one wall and she assumed it was some sort of two-way mirror that allowed people to see into the room.

She was left alone, and, as she sat at the table, the first real wave of emotion struck her. Pain. It seared through her heart.

A fool. She'd been such a fool. Initially she'd been afraid Nick was using her to get closer to her uncle, to gain a more favorable position in Jonas's employment.

In the time they'd spent together, he'd assuaged those worries, seducing her into believing that his only reason for spending time with her, sharing moments with her, was that he liked her, he wanted her.

And she'd taken the bait, hook, line and sinker. An aching bereavement shot through her as she realized it had all been false. Every heated glance he had given to her, every special word he had spoken to her, every touch and kiss he'd shared with her had been lies, all lies.

Tears once again burned at her eyes, and she

swiped at them angrily. He didn't deserve her tears. He was a liar, a deceiver.

She had no idea what was going on for sure. Had this been about trapping her, concerning the robberies? She leaned back in the chair and rubbed her fingers across her forehead. Think. She had to think. She had to somehow make sense of all this.

Looking back now over the past two weeks they had shared, she realized how often he'd asked her little things about Jonas, about where he was, what he was doing. His casual questions had seemed benign at the time, but now nothing that had occurred in the past two weeks seemed benign.

Why had he been using her? What had he wanted from her? Information about Jonas, or had he been trying to entrap her for the robberies?

Thank God she hadn't shared her innermost secrets with him. Thank God Jonas had spent her lifetime warning her about people like Nick.

But that didn't make his betrayal any less painful.

She stared at the door, waiting impatiently for somebody to come in and speak with her. She needed to make a phone call to let Jonas know what had happened. He would straighten this out. She was certain it was just a matter of time and she'd be released.

At least they'd removed the cuffs. She rubbed her reddened wrists absently. She couldn't wait to get out of here and when she did, she'd never see or speak to Nick Barnes again. Certainly he could be assured his job as head of security for Jonas was over. Not that losing his job there would probably bother him. After all, he was apparently a hotshot FBI agent.

What was his game? Why had he been working for Jonas? Obviously he'd been undercover, but why? At the moment nothing made sense except the pain that ripped through her heart.

He'd used her. For the first time in her life she'd allowed a man to get close to her, had let down her guard and had trusted like she'd never done before.

She closed her eyes, remembering each touch of his hand, every word he'd uttered to her, the fire of every kiss they had shared. Lies. All lies.

The pain inside her transformed to a rich cold anger. She opened her eyes as she heard the door to the room open. She frowned as Nick walked in and closed the door behind him.

"Get somebody else in here to talk to me, because I'm not talking to you," she said, her voice thick with the anger that rippled inside her.

He ignored her words and seated himself opposite her at the table. "Why don't you tell me what in the hell you were doing tonight?"

She wanted to scream at him, ask him what in the hell she thought *he* was doing, but she refused to give him the satisfaction of seeing how utterly devastated she was by his subterfuge. "It's complicated," she said, refusing to meet his gaze.

"Well, uncomplicate it for me." There was a toughness in his voice she'd never heard before.

"I'd like to make my phone call, then all of this will be straightened out," she replied.

"I don't think you recognize how much trouble you're in, Lynn. You're facing felony theft charges, along with a multitude of other charges. No phone call from anyone is going to straighten this out."

She looked at him then and raised her chin in a show of defiance. "Trust me, you're all going to have egg on your face when Uncle Jonas talks to his government contact."

He stared at her as if she were speaking a foreign language. "What government contact?"

"If you just let me call Uncle Jonas, then he can explain it all to you. This is all one big mistake. I'm not a thief, there's just been some sort of mix-up."

He slammed his hands down on the table. She jumped at the force of his action. "I don't want Jonas to explain anything to me. I want you to talk to me. We have over a dozen thefts on the books, and right now you're looking good for all of them. I want to know what in the hell you think you've been doing."

She jumped up, the chair skittering backward on the floor as something snapped inside her. "Why don't you tell me what in the hell you think you've been doing, *Agent* Barnes?" She was appalled by the tremble that seemed to take possession of her voice. "Why don't you tell me what kind of game you've been playing?"

For a moment the air between them crackled with tension, with the acrid scent of broken trust and the simmering rage of betrayal. "Tell me what you were doing, Agent Barnes, working for Uncle Jonas. Tell me why you're on our payroll as a security expert when you have such a prominent position with the FBI. Tell me what you were doing every time you held me in your arms and kissed me."

The words fired from her and the tremble that had been in her voice disappeared beneath the cold, hard anger that ripped through her. "You get me a phone so I can make my phone call, and beyond that I don't have anything else to say to you."

She sat back down, folded her hands and glared at him.

A muscle ticked ominously in his jaw. He stood and pulled his cell phone from his pocket. "Make your call. I'll wait outside." He set the phone on the table, then turned and left the room.

The moment he left the room the anger that had sustained her vanished, leaving in its wake a heart heaviness she'd never known before.

He hadn't answered any of her questions. She still had no idea why he'd been working for Jonas. More important, she had no idea why he'd worked to get so close to her, what he could possibly want from her.

She picked up the phone and dialed Jonas's number, praying that he would answer. As she'd feared, it went directly to voice mail.

"Uncle Jonas, it's me." She paused a few seconds, then continued. "I went after the urn tonight and I've been arrested by the FBI. I'm at the South Patrol precinct. You need to talk to your contact and get me out of here. Please, Uncle Jonas…get me out of here as soon as possible."

She clicked off and set the phone down on the table. How long would it be before Jonas checked his voice mail? Even on those rare occasions that he told her he would be incommunicado, he'd always assured her that he listened to his voice mail frequently and would always be available should she need him.

She needed him now. This room, this place, was getting to her. She could smell the odor of the people who had sat at this table before her. The stench of sweat and fear permeated the room.

A surge of panic swept through her and she grabbed the phone and once again punched in Jonas's number. "Uncle Jonas, please hurry and call me as soon as you get this message. I need you." She read off the number from Nick's cell phone, then disconnected.

She remained in the room by herself for what

seemed like an eternity, staring at the phone and willing it to ring. She looked up as the door opened and Nick walked back in.

He sank down in the chair across from her and for a moment they sat in silence, their gazes locked. As Lynn stared at his familiar features, she realized the depth of her emotional involvement with him.

She'd been perilously close to falling in love with him, and this recognition refired the flames of her rage. It had felt so real with him, but she realized now that her relationship with him had been no more real than the cyberspace relationships she shared through the Internet.

"Did you get in touch with Jonas?" he finally asked.

She shook her head. "I left a message for him. I also gave him your phone number. I'm sure he'll be calling very soon."

"Are you going to tell me why a woman who has everything she could want would spend her nights stealing antiquities and jewels?" he asked. There was no anger in his voice this time. Instead there was a deep weariness. "I'd really like to understand. Can you explain it to me?"

"I don't owe you any explanations," she said with a forced coolness.

His lips thinned. "Perhaps you'll feel more like talking after spending a night in jail."

"I shouldn't be here more than an hour or two," she said with a burst of confidence. She stood. "Take me to a cell. I'd prefer to cool my heels there than in your company."

"Lynn, let me explain—"

"I don't want to hear any explanations," she said, interrupting whatever he was about to say. No explanation he could offer could take away what he had done. He'd taken her emotions, all her trust and abused them in the worst possible way.

"Fine." The muscle once again ticked in his jaw as he stood and left the room. A moment later a uniformed police officer came into the room to escort her to her accommodations for the night.

Lynn had never been in a police station in her life. As the officer walked her toward the back of the building, she noted that this particular station house was smaller than she would have guessed most police stations to be.

It was housed in an old brick building, and she fought a shudder as she anticipated the cell where she'd be spending the next couple of hours or so.

There was absolutely no doubt in her mind that her uncle Jonas would move heaven and earth to get her out as soon as possible. All she had to do was endure until he made the appropriate arrangements.

The cell she was led to wasn't as bad as she'd anticipated. Although small, containing only two bunks and a stool and sink, everything appeared to be clean. The clang of the cell door resounded in her head, and when the officer disappeared she was utterly alone.

The only sound was the slow, steady drip of the sink faucet and the screaming inside her own head. She could deal with being locked up for a couple of hours, she had even dealt with the indignity of being fingerprinted and having mug shots taken, but what she was finding impossible to resolve were her feelings about Nick.

Why had he done what he'd done? What had he gained by pretending to like her, pretending to desire her? Why had he been working for her Uncle Jonas? It wasn't as if he'd just been hired recently. He'd worked for Jonas for the past two years. None of it made any sense.

She climbed onto the upper bunk, leaned her back against the wall and pulled her legs up to her chest. She'd never known heartache before now.

She felt stupid and naive. Whenever she'd been with Nick she'd listened with her heart, not her head. She'd forgotten all the things Jonas had warned her about and had allowed herself to be taken advantage of.

Never again. Never again would she trust as easily. Never again would she believe the sweet-talk of any man. She'd actually contemplated sharing with Nick the secrets of her physical gifts. Thank God she hadn't, for she had no idea what he might have done with that information.

The minutes ticked by with excruciating slowness. Her thoughts flittered in confusion as she waited for her godfather to rescue her.

Her mind played back in great detail each and every moment she'd spent with Nick. Her cheeks burned as she thought of how close she'd come to sleeping with him.

She had no idea when she fell asleep, but she awakened with a start. Across the hallway from her cell, a window showed the first light of dawn.

Dawn? How could it be dawn? Where had the night gone?

She unkinked from her position, her muscles aching from too much time cramped up. She slid to the floor and stretched, the first stir of disquiet sweeping through her.

Why hadn't she been released? Surely Uncle Jonas had gotten her messages by now. How long could it take to let the people in charge know that she wasn't a common thief but rather had been working for the government?

She thought of the doubts she'd entertained concerning the work she'd been doing, doubts that now seemed bigger and stronger than ever. She refused to entertain those doubts. She had to believe in Jonas. She had to believe there was a logical reason why she was still behind bars.

She used the facilities, grateful that no guard was leering at her, then washed her face and hands at the sink, then sat on the bottom bunk to wait for what happened next. She didn't have long to wait.

Within an hour an officer came to get her and led her back into the room where she'd been held the night before. She sat at the table and prepared herself for whatever might come.

She was unsurprised when Nick came into the room. He carried two foam cups of coffee and a file folder. Even though she wanted nothing to do with him, her need for creature comfort won out as she reached for one of the cups of coffee.

"You didn't want to listen to me last night, but you're going to listen to me now," he said as he sat at the table. "I've been undercover for the past two years, working for Jonas in an attempt to gain access to information that would put him behind bars for the rest of his life."

She looked at him in surprise. "For what?"

His ruggedly handsome features were drawn and taut. He looked as if he'd gotten considerably less sleep than she had. "Lynn, your godfather isn't the man you think he is. We've linked him to a worldwide smuggling network. He deals in illegal drugs and weapons. He uses the black market to sell artwork, antiquities and jewels that we now believe you have obtained for him."

"That's not true," she replied in a hoarse whisper, appalled by what he'd said. "The things I retrieved from museums and other places, they weren't for Jonas. They were for the government. Jonas works for a government agency to help in the recovery of stolen items. I get them, then they are returned to their rightful owners."

He stared at her for a long moment and in the depth of his dark brown eyes she saw a whisper of pity. "Lynn, there is no government agency. Just like there are no defense contracts. Jonas White is a criminal. He supplies terrorists with weapons, he manipulates people for his amusement and monetary gain. When you took those items and gave them to Jonas, they immediately went up for sale on the black market and he put the money he got into his bank accounts. He used you, Lynn."

"I don't believe you." Her voice was barely audible. She felt as if she'd been sucker punched and all the air in her body had been violently slammed out of her.

"Why should I believe you? You're the one who used me."

It was much easier for her to focus on his betrayal than to even contemplate that what he said about Jonas might be true.

Nick leaned back in the chair and swept a hand through his thick, dark hair. "You're right. Part of my job was to seduce you and find out what I could about Jonas's illegal activities."

She'd guessed it, but the words, so stark and bold, were like arrows into her heart. Once again she felt the hot press of tears burning at her eyes, but she swallowed hard against them. It had been his job. Every kiss, every touch, every heated glance had been nothing more than a job to him.

He leaned forward, usurping his half of the small table and venturing onto her half. "Lynn, I know you probably won't believe a word that comes out of my mouth right now, but I want you to understand something. I went into this assignment thinking I had a job to do. Within hours of spending time with you things got complicated, because it was no longer just a job."

He reached a hand across the table and touched the back of hers. She drew hers away, not wanting him to touch her when her head was filled with such chaos. She knew she would find even the most casual touch from him excruciatingly painful.

He sighed and pulled his hand back. "Trying to get information about Jonas from you was my job. But when I kissed you, when I danced with you and held you close, I forgot all about the job. I realized I just wanted to be with you."

It would be a wonderful balm to her aching heart if she could believe him. She rubbed the center of her forehead with trembling fingers. "At the moment I don't know what to believe," she finally said.

"Believe this. Jonas can't get you out of this. There isn't going to be some magical phone call from a government agency telling us that you work for them. You're in deep trouble here, and you are the only person who can help yourself."

"What do you mean?"

"We don't want you, Lynn. We never wanted you. We want Jonas. And we know that you can bring him to us."

A headache banged at her temples. "How am I supposed to do that?" she asked.

"We need his payroll and other financial records. It's the last piece we're lacking in making our case against him. We need you to confirm that Jonas was behind the robberies. You get those records for us and go on record that he told you to steal those items and we'll drop all charges against you. You can walk away from here without any record that you were ever arrested."

So, he wanted her to betray the man who had raised her, the man who had taken her into his home as a baby and had given her a life of love and care.

How could she possibly justify doing such a thing to the man who had been like a father to her? How could she possibly believe that Jonas was the kind of man he'd described to her?

"Lynn, I know I've thrown a lot at you in the last few minutes, and I know I've given you no reason whatsoever to trust anything I say to you." His eyes were beguiling and she averted her gaze from his, unable to continue to look at him.

"There's been no phone call, Lynn. I had the phone with me all night long. Jonas isn't going to call and save you. He's hung you out to dry."

She rubbed her forehead once again and frowned. "Maybe he hasn't gotten my message yet. Maybe he's traveling and can't use his phone or can't get hold of his contact." She desperately wanted, needed to believe either scenario.

Nick didn't reply. Instead he pushed the file folder he'd carried in across the table in front of her, then stood. "That's background information on your godfather. I'll give you some time to go through it, then we'll talk again."

He walked over to the door, then turned back to look at her once again. "Lynn, maybe I lied about who I was, but I didn't lie about how I feel about you. We have something special between us. The last thing I want to do is hurt you." With these words he turned and left the room.

She stared after him, emotions warring in her soul. Something special. That's what she'd felt as well. She wanted to believe what he said, but couldn't forget that ultimately he wanted something from her. He wanted Jonas.

She looked down at the file folder on the table, almost afraid to open it. Like Pandora's box she feared what might escape and how it would affect the life she believed she'd had.

With an enormous sense of dread she pulled the folder closer and opened it.

She had no idea how long she sat there alone, reading about the man who had taken her in, lavished her with gifts and created the only family she knew.

She learned that her godfather had been born Johannes Bianco and had grown up on the streets of New York just outside of Hell's Kitchen. His mother had been killed in a mob shooting when he'd been ten and he'd lived with his stepfather until he'd turned sixteen and struck out on his own.

It was sometime during the next several years that he changed his name to Jonas White and, according to the information in the file, began a life of crime.

The crimes they suspected him of doing stole her breath away. Drug smuggling, arms dealing and black-market trade were only part of what they believed he was involved in.

When she finally closed the file folder, her headache had grown to mammoth proportions. She wanted to escape from all of this…the jail, Nick and the information she'd just read.

If she believed everything that was in that file, then nothing in her life had been real or good. If she believed what she'd just read, then that meant Jonas had trained her, lied to her and made her one of the best thieves around in order to further his personal wealth.

If she believed what she'd just read, then she was left with nothing to hold on to, nothing whatsoever to believe in. If she believed what she'd read then her entire life had been built on lies.

A thunderous roar shook the building. She jumped up from the table as tiny pieces of sheetrock rained down and dust filled the air.

From outside the room she could hear the excited shouting of men and the slap of running footsteps. What had happened? What was going on?

The door to the room flew open and a young woman stepped inside. She was clad all in black, her golden blond hair a startling contrast to her dark clothes. She grabbed Lynn by the arm. "Come on, let's go."

Lynn had no idea who the woman was, but it was obvious she wasn't an officer of the law. She ripped her arm from the woman's hold. "What's going on? What's happening?"

"We don't have time for that now. Let's get out of here," the woman said. Once again she grabbed hold of Lynn and attempted to pull her through the doorway.

Lynn shoved the woman away from her. She had no idea what was happening. She was tired, confused and more than a little bit cranky. She certainly wasn't going to let some mysterious woman drag her anywhere.

The woman's pretty features pulled into a frown and she lunged for Lynn. Adrenaline spiked through Lynn. The lunge was overly aggressive and Lynn countered with aggression of her own.

She sidestepped the woman then kicked out, a high kick that the woman deflected with her arm. Lynn had the feeling that the world had gone mad as they began to grapple in earnest.

She was fighting a woman she'd never seen before, a woman whose physical skills seemed to match her own. Her kicks were as fast, as high as Lynn's and she moved with an agility to rival Lynn's.

Who was this woman and why did she want Lynn to go with her? Questions screamed in Lynn's head, but she was too busy fighting to worry about answers.

As the woman attempted to get Lynn into a head-lock and drag her toward the door, Lynn used every ounce of skill she possessed to flip the woman onto the floor on her back.

"Who are you and what do you want from me?" Lynn asked breathlessly as she stared down at the pretty woman.

Unusual green-gold eyes stared up at her, eyes that looked hauntingly familiar, eyes Lynn saw each time she looked into the mirror.

"I'm Dawn. I'm your sister, Lynn, and we've got to get you out of here."

Chapter 11

Her sister?

Lynn felt as if she'd entered an alternate reality. As the woman—Dawn—held out her hand, Lynn made an instantaneous decision. She reached for the outstretched hand, grabbed it tight and pulled Dawn up from the floor.

At that moment another roar ripped through the air and more shouts erupted in the hallway.

"Come on, we've lost precious time." Still holding her hand, Dawn pulled her out the door and into chaos. Uniformed officers ran in all directions, paying no attention to the two women as they made their way toward the back of the building. The sound of sirens rent the air.

Dawn led her to a door, and they burst through it and into the early-morning sunshine. As Dawn took off running down the sidewalk, Lynn followed, surprised by the speed Dawn displayed.

They ran for two blocks, then Dawn stopped at the driver's-side door of a sports car. "Get in," she said, and gestured toward the passenger door.

Lynn slid in and said nothing as Dawn started the engine and pulled away from the curb. She had no idea what she was doing. She had no idea if coming with Dawn had been a mistake or not. She was functioning on sheer adrenaline.

It wasn't until they were some distance from the police station that she turned to Dawn. "What happened back there?"

"I created a few little diversions so I could get in and get you out."

"What kind of diversions?"

"A few bombs carefully placed so they wouldn't kill anyone, but would cause enough havoc that I could get you out."

Bombs. Could things get any worse? "Are you going to tell me what's going on?"

"Not now. First we need to stash you someplace safe, then I'll explain everything."

Lynn leaned her head back against the headrest

and closed her eyes. She felt as if too much information had been pumped into her brain in the past twelve hours.

Nick's betrayal. Jonas's suspected crimes. And now this woman breaking her out of jail and claiming to be her sister. It all jumbled together in her head, creating a feeling of overload.

She opened her eyes and stared at the woman who sat in the driver's seat, a woman who claimed to be her sister. How was that possible? According to Jonas, Lynn had been the only child of a couple who had died at sea. He'd been her godfather and had adopted her when she'd been five months old.

If she believed Jonas, then there was no way she could have a sister. If she believed...

"Dawn what?" she asked.

"Dawn O'Shaughnessy." She cast Lynn a quick smile. "I know you're confused, Lynn. I promise you I'll tell you everything just as soon as we get to the motel."

"The motel?"

Dawn nodded. "I've got a room at a motel not far from here. Once we get settled in there I'll explain everything to you."

That was fine with Lynn. She didn't think she could stand any more surprises at the moment. She was not only exhausted, hungry and confused, she was also now a fugitive from justice.

The thought gave her chills. Even if she was eventually cleared of the charges for the robberies, she now faced other charges equally as serious.

She was grateful when Dawn drove through a fast-food drive-in and ordered burgers, fries and soft drinks. A block from the fast-food restaurant she pulled into the Sleepy Time Motel and in front of unit 101.

Minutes later the two sat across from each other at a small table inside the motel room, the food on the table before them. "Eat first, then we'll talk," Dawn said.

Lynn unwrapped her burger. "We'll talk while we eat," she countered. She stared at Dawn in open curiosity. Dawn returned the gaze, as if taking stock of exactly what she'd pulled out of the police station.

"I was told that my parents were eccentric millionaires who died in a boating accident when I was five months old," Lynn began.

"You were told a pack of lies," Dawn replied. Her eyes, so like Lynn's in shape and hue, held secrets Lynn wasn't sure she wanted to know.

If Jonas had lied to her about who her parents were and how they had died, then she had to face the fact that he'd lied to her about other things. She had to face the possibility that Nick had told her the truth about the man who had raised her. The thought sent a chill of despair through her.

"Then tell me the truth," she said to Dawn, although she wasn't sure she'd know the truth if it bit her on the butt.

"It's a long, complicated story," Dawn warned her.

"I'm not going anywhere," Lynn replied dryly.

As they ate, Dawn began an incredible tale about a woman named Lorraine Miller Carrington. Rainy, as she had been called, according to Dawn, had years before been a student at the Athena Academy for the Advancement of Women, in Arizona.

The school was located just outside of the Glendale/Phoenix area at the base of the White Tank Mountains. The school had caught the interest of Lab 33, a top-secret government facility located in the middle of nowhere in New Mexico.

Dawn explained to Lynn that she, herself, was born and raised at Lab 33 and had only left the lab recently to search for some answers she needed, and to search for the sibling she was certain existed.

"But what does this have to do with you and me being sisters? I've never heard of Rainy or Athena Academy or Lab 33 before," Lynn said. "This has to be a big mistake. What makes you think we could be sisters?"

"I don't think. I know," Dawn replied with certainty. "When Rainy was a student at Athena Academy, she underwent what she thought was an emergency appendectomy. What really happened was

that eggs were taken from her. You see, Aldrich Pe-
ters, one of the men in charge of Lab 33, wanted to
see if he could create genetically enhanced fe-
males...superfemales."

Lynn thought of her tremendous strength and
agility and her enhanced senses, which Jonas had always told her were gifts from nature. Her heartbeat
quickened and she shoved the last of her hamburger
and fries aside, her appetite gone.

"What happened next?" She felt as if she were
hearing a fantastic, science-fiction kind of story, one
that had nothing to do with her.

"Ads were placed in newspapers to look for suit-
able surrogate mothers, and the embryos were implanted in these women."

"What about Rainy? What happened to her?" Lynn
asked, her mind reeling with each new bit of information that was exposed.

Dawn's eyes darkened and her lips compressed
into a grim line. "She died almost a year ago. Initially
it was thought she fell asleep at the wheel of her car,
but we now know she was murdered. Her death began
all this. Rainy had several close schoolmates from
Athena, and when she died, these women became de-
termined to find out the truth."

"And the truth is?"

"You and I are the products of a genetic experiment."

Even though Lynn knew where the conversation had been headed, to hear these words spoken aloud shook her. "But I don't understand. If that's true, then how did I end up with Uncle Jonas? Is he part of Lab 33?"

Dawn took a sip of her soda, then carefully folded up the empty wrapper from her burger and placed it back into the sack. "One of the surrogates was a woman named Cleo Patra."

Lynn looked at her dubiously. "Cleo Patra?"

"I'm not lying, that's her name. She was a Vegas showgirl. Anyway she agreed to be a surrogate and was implanted. When she went into labor and was being taken to the hospital, she and her doctor were waylaid by a man and taken to a warehouse. Cleo gave birth to a little girl, but the baby was stolen from her that night. Cleo's life was threatened and the man and the baby disappeared."

"The man was Jonas?" Lynn felt sick as she thought of the man she loved, the man who had raised her.

"No. From the description Cleo gave me of the man, I believe it was Richard Dunst who stole the baby and gave her to Jonas White. Dunst was a drinking buddy of a Lab 33 scientist, the man who infiltrated Athena Academy and handpicked our biological mother to be the egg donor. His name is—was—Carl Bradford. Dunst's connections to Bradford and Jonas are what led me to you."

Lynn leaned back in her chair as the final nail in Jonas's coffin was pounded in. "And that baby was me," she said flatly.

Dawn nodded. "We believe Dunst told Jonas about the secret genetic experiments that Lab 33 was conducting, and Jonas decided he wanted one of the superbabies."

"I became the perfect tool for him," Lynn said bitterly. "I stole for him." She felt sick as the full ramifications of it all filled her head. "He raised me solely for the purpose of being a thief for him." Nick had been right. There wouldn't have been a phone call to help her out of her jam with the FBI.

She looked at Dawn once again. "It was you who tried to break into Jonas's house, wasn't it? It was you I chased across the lawn."

"Yeah. I'd been watching you for a couple of weeks. I wanted to make sure I hadn't made a mistake. The night that I tried to break in I was going to talk to you, but the glass made more noise than I anticipated and I was afraid of getting caught by your security, so I freaked and ran."

At least Lynn knew now she wasn't crazy, that somebody had been watching her.

Dawn took another sip of her soda, then frowned at Lynn. Lynn steeled herself, knowing there was more to come.

"Like you, I have unusual strength and agility, but I also got another ability. I have superhealing genes."

Lynn stared at her skeptically. "It's true," Dawn exclaimed.

As Lynn watched, Dawn withdrew a small penknife from her pocket. She opened the knife then drew the blade across her wrist. Lynn gasped as blood welled up in the wound.

"Are you crazy?" Lynn said, and fumbled on the table looking for napkins or something to use to stanch the flow of blood.

However, before she could find anything, the bleeding stopped and the wound began to close itself. Lynn grabbed Dawn's hand and pulled it closer to her, staring down at the place where Dawn had cut herself. It was completely healed with no sign of the wound she'd just seen.

If she'd needed any proof of the incredible story Dawn had just told her, she had that proof now. She closed her hand over Dawn's. A sister. She had a sister. "When I was little I used to fantasize about having a sister," she said, surprised by the emotion that suddenly clogged her throat.

Dawn squeezed her hand. "It isn't a fantasy anymore, Lynn. We're sisters, and we have a lot of catching up to do. I want you to come with me, to meet the Athenas—the women who were closest to our mother." Dawn squeezed her hand once again, then released it and stood. "I know I've hit you with a lot. I understand you need some time."

She looked at her wristwatch. "I've got some things to take care of and will be gone for several hours. There's food in the mini refrigerator, and the microwave works. You're welcome to anything you can find."

She walked over to the dresser and grabbed a small notepad and pen. "I'm giving you my cell phone number. Call me if you need me for anything, otherwise I'll be back later this afternoon."

Lynn stood and followed her to the door. "I just need some time to digest all this."

"I understand, but Lynn, don't take too long. We need to get you out of here and I'm eager to introduce you to Rainy's friends." Dawn wrapped Lynn in an embrace. "I didn't find my sister just to lose her," she said fiercely.

Lynn returned the embrace, her heart welcoming in the warmth of this new connection, this family bond she'd never known existed.

Dawn slipped out the door, and Lynn closed and locked it behind her. For a moment she leaned against the door, completely overwhelmed by everything that had happened.

The few hours of sleep she'd gotten seemed long ago and not nearly enough to sustain her as she worked to make sense of everything that had happened.

Maybe after a few hours of sleep her head would

be clearer, she thought. She crawled into one of the two beds the room held and closed her eyes.

If she believed Dawn, she was the result of an experiment, and she had no parents who had drowned at sea. Jonas had been responsible for her being kidnapped from the woman who had given birth to her. Round and round it all whirled in her head until finally she fell into an exhausted sleep.

She dreamed that she was back in Sensations, drinking Alabama Slammers with her friends, but every time she tried to take a drink her cell phone rang and Jonas yelled at her to get home. Then Dawn burst in and threw Lynn over her shoulder and carried her toward the exit. As they went out the door, she saw Nick calling after them, his eyes filled with regret and pity.

She awakened with a gasp and sat up, for a moment disoriented as to her surroundings. Then she remembered. She was a fugitive from the law, hiding out in a motel room rented by a sister she'd never known she had.

The clock on the nightstand told her it was almost four in the afternoon. She raked her fingers through her hair and got out of the bed. What she needed now was a shower to wash away the stink of the jail. Hopefully a hot shower would also clear her mind.

A satchel with some clothes sat on the dresser. Lynn assumed they belonged to Dawn. She hoped her sister wouldn't mind if she borrowed some items. The two women were about the same size, and Lynn couldn't stand the idea of showering, then putting on the same clothes.

She found a T-shirt and a pair of jeans and she carried them with her into the bathroom. Minutes later, clean and rested, she looked in the mini refrigerator for something to eat. She grabbed a store-prepared chicken sandwich and a soda, then sat at the table to eat and to think.

She was a fugitive. The police, the FBI, they would all be looking for her. New charges would certainly be added to the ones she already faced. From here on out, she would forever live her life looking over her shoulder, waiting to be rearrested for the crimes she had committed.

Crimes she had committed. Her heart constricted as she thought of all the precious items she had stolen, then handed to Jonas. She'd believed she was helping the government. She'd believed she was doing something good. It killed her to recognize there had been nothing good in any of it.

She'd not only been incredibly naive, she must have been positively comatose. She'd had questions. She'd had concerns, but she'd shoved them aside, listening to Jonas when she should have been listening to her instincts.

Her entire life with Jonas had been nothing more

than a pack of lies. If she believed what Dawn told her, then Jonas and Richard Dunst had stolen her when she'd been a baby, specifically in order to exploit her unusual abilities.

Jonas had kept her isolated and filled with fears from the time she'd been a small child. Of course he hadn't wanted her to get close to anyone. He'd been afraid of questions, afraid that somebody else's involvement with her might complicate his manipulation of her.

Then there was Dawn. The story she'd told Lynn had been truly incredible…an evil lab and human experiments. It would have been easy for Lynn to reject the entire thing had she not seen with her own eyes the immediate healing of the wound on Dawn's wrist.

Besides, as crazy as it sounded, when she'd looked into Dawn's eyes—eyes that were so much like her own—she'd felt a strange connection. She wasn't sure if it was because she so wanted to believe that Dawn was her sister, or if there was truly a kind of mystical link between siblings.

In any case, she believed Dawn, and she wanted to learn more about Lorraine Miller Carrington and the Athena Academy.

Finally there was Nick, who had used her to gain information about Jonas. Who had told her he hadn't meant to hurt her with his deception, that getting close to her had been more than a job.

She finished the sandwich and got up from the table. Thoughts of Nick hurt. She walked over to the window and pulled the thick curtain aside.

She had no idea where this particular motel was located. She'd never been to this area of Miami before. She let the curtain fall back into place and sat on the edge of the bed, her thoughts still consumed with Nick.

He'd made her feel so special when he'd gazed at her with those soulful dark eyes of his. His kisses had been filled with desire, or at least that's what she'd thought. She'd believed everything he'd shared with her. She'd believed he'd cared about her. She'd cared about him.

But how could she believe him now? How could she believe him when he told her it had been more than a job, that he did care about her? He still wanted something from her. He wanted her to help put Jonas behind bars for the rest of his life.

And she wasn't at all sure she could do that. She needed to talk to Jonas. Even though the evidence she'd been shown and had been told pointed to him being a man who had lived outside the law for many years, she couldn't forget all that he'd done for her.

She knew another man, one who had been a philanthropist, who had given money to all kinds of charitable organizations. She knew a man who had hugged her when she'd been frightened, made her laugh when she'd been sad. He'd given her the best education money could buy and a life of luxury that many would envy.

She realized she couldn't make a decision to help Nick until she spoke with Jonas. She certainly couldn't leave here to go with Dawn until she spoke with him. Somehow she needed to make contact with him.

There was only one person she knew who could get her in contact with her godfather. Richard Dunst…the man who had kidnapped her as a baby and threatened the woman who had given birth to her.

The sound of a key at the door forced her off the bed and into a defensive stance. She relaxed as Dawn stepped in. "I borrowed some of your clothes. I hope you don't mind."

Dawn flashed her a smile. "No, I don't mind." Her smile faded, and she eyed Lynn with obvious concern. "Are you okay?"

Lynn sank back down on the edge of the bed. "I don't know. I got a couple hours of sleep, but my head is still reeling with everything that's happened."

"Have you made a decision? Will you come with me?"

"Yes, I'll go with you. But there are some things I have to take care of first." Lynn explained to Dawn about the FBI wanting her to help them put Jonas behind bars. "I need to talk to Jonas," she said. "And in order to do that I need to borrow your car."

"All right, but what are you going to do? How are you going to get in contact with Jonas?" Dawn asked.

"I'm going to call Richard Dunst and meet him someplace."

Dawn's eyes darkened, turning more green than gold. "That man is evil, Lynn."

"He won't hurt me," Lynn said with a certainty she didn't feel. "This is something I have to do. I feel like I've spent all my life being manipulated and used by everyone around me."

She stood up and paced the carpet. "Now I intend to take control of my own life. I need answers and I'm not going to stop until I get them." Lynn felt the strength flowing through her, a strength she'd never felt before. A swell of excitement welled up inside Lynn as she realized she was about to take her destiny into her own hands.

Dawn gazed at her for a long moment. "Okay. Tell me what I can do to help you."

Chapter 12

It had taken a single phone call to Richard Dunst to arrange a meeting between Lynn and the bald, expressionless man who had always given her the creeps.

It was impossible to set up a meeting in a public place because Lynn had no idea what news stories had broken about the explosions at the police station and her subsequent escape. There was no way she wanted to chance being seen in a public place, so she and Dunst agreed to meet at a warehouse Jonas owned near the docks.

Dawn wanted to go with her, but Lynn insisted she had to go alone. For too long Lynn had been dependent on others. She'd allowed herself to be led without standing on her own two feet. She needed to do this alone.

The meeting time was set for nine that evening. At eight-thirty Lynn left the motel room. She wore a baseball cap covering her hair and pulled down low to shield her features, and she was armed with a knife that Dawn insisted she take with her in case of trouble.

Lynn wasn't expecting trouble. There was no reason for Dunst to want to harm her. All she wanted from him was to find out where Jonas was and how she could get in touch with him. She had to talk to Jonas one last time before she made a decision about betraying him.

She'd been to the warehouse where she was meeting Dunst several times in the past. The warehouse was one of several that contained Jonas's overstock from his import/export business.

Dusk fell in deep purple shadows as she pulled up to the warehouse. Dunst's car was already parked in front of the building.

She sat in the car for a moment, gathering her strength, her thoughts. She was about to face the man who, according to Dawn, had stolen her and presented her like a gift to Jonas.

She got out of the car, her hand tracing the length of the knife in her pocket. The burgeoning strength she'd felt at the motel with Dawn had only grown stronger with each passing minute.

Lynn had always been confident of her physical skills, but this was the first time she felt empowered by her own mental and emotional strength. For years Jonas had called her his baby, but she wasn't a baby. She was a woman with special gifts, a woman who was just beginning to understand the magnitude of her abilities and choices.

The warehouse was unlocked and she walked in and went directly to the office, where Richard Dunst sat at the desk in the small, airless room.

As she walked in he rose and came around the front of the desk. "Lynn, thank God you called me when you did." To her surprise he reached out and took her hand in his. "Jonas and I have been worried sick about you."

Lynn pulled her hand from his. "I called Jonas from jail twice last night. Why didn't he call me back?" She realized that what she wanted more than anything was a logical explanation, a reason to believe that all the things Nick had told her about her godfather were lies.

She wanted to believe that Dawn was mistaken about where Lynn had come from, how she had come to be a part of Jonas's family. She wanted to believe in the man who had been her surrogate parent. She desperately wanted to believe that Jonas was the man she had thought he was.

"I'm afraid it's a difficult matter," Richard said and returned to his seat behind the desk.

A difficult matter. A complicated situation. Those were the same kinds of words Jonas had always used to explain what they'd been doing for the government. They were words that answered nothing.

"I don't understand what's difficult about it," she replied as she sank into the chair opposite the desk. "He told me all he had to do was make a phone call to his government contact and I would be released."

"How did you manage to escape?" Richard asked, obviously ignoring what she'd just said.

"That isn't important. Why didn't Uncle Jonas get me out of jail last night? He had plenty of time to arrange for my release."

Richard's shaved head shone in the harsh artificial light overhead, and his hazel eyes glittered brightly. She thought of what Dawn had said about him, that he was an evil man. For the first time she felt his evil, smelled it in the air emanating from him, saw it in the cold, brittle shine of his eyes.

"Lynnette, your uncle Jonas has been betrayed by his contact. He's in hiding here in Miami and plans to fly to Puerto Isla as soon as possible. He wants you to go with him. I can take you to him right now."

It would have been easy for her to take his words at face value. The old Lynn would have accepted Richard's explanation without question. But in the past twenty-four hours, Lynn had undergone a transformation of growth and inner strength.

She now saw the cold calculation in Richard's gaze. She also realized from his words that Jonas wasn't out of the country as she had believed the night before. He was right here in Miami.

"Go to Puerto Isla?" She feigned confusion. "I can't make a decision about going anywhere unless I talk to Uncle Jonas," she said.

"You don't have many choices. You're a fugitive, Lynn. The best thing for both you and Jonas is to get out of the country, and Puerto Isla has no extradition laws."

"I still need some time to think," she said firmly. "So much has happened."

"Lynnette, I don't know what the police might have told you, but whatever it was you can be certain it was lies. I certainly hope you didn't talk to them about your special talents or your work with Jonas."

"I refused to speak to them at all," she replied.

"Good. Jonas loves you and he's quite impressed with the way you got away from the jail."

A cold hard knot formed in her chest. What kind of man was impressed when somebody he loved broke out of jail and became a fugitive from justice? Certainly not a man who valued the difference between right and wrong. Certainly not a man who was innocent of doing anything illegal.

Richard stood once again. "I can take you to him right now, Lynnette. We can be out of the country in a matter of hours."

"I want to talk to him first. Give me a phone number where I can reach him," she said.

Richard's eyes flashed darkly, although his mask-like features betrayed nothing of his emotions. He grabbed a scrap of paper from the desk and scribbled down a number, then held it out to her. "You'd better call him soon. He can't wait around for you forever. It's imperative that he leave the country as soon as possible."

Minutes later, as she drove Dawn's car back toward the motel room, she once again thought of all the information she'd seen about Jonas in the file Nick had given her to read.

All they needed to arrest Jonas was her telling them that Jonas had been the mastermind behind the thefts. If she gave them his financial records she had no doubt that they would be able to link him to any number of crimes. In all probability he would spend the rest of his life behind bars.

Even if Jonas deserved whatever the judicial system handed him, that didn't make betraying him any easier.

Dawn waited for her at the motel. "How did it go?" she asked when Lynn walked through the door.

"Okay. I got a number for Jonas from Dunst." Lynn

handed the car keys to Dawn. "It was so hard to look at him and know that he was the one who stole me from Cleo Patra. I always thought Richard was creepy, but now I know he's evil."

"You don't know the half of it," Dawn replied. "I don't think any of us knows the extent of Richard Dunst's evilness. So, are you ready to come with me?"

"I can't, Dawn. At least, not right now." Lynn sat on the edge of the bed and realized that at some point on the drive back to the motel room she'd come to a decision. "I want to clear my name before I do anything else. I need to get in touch with the authorities and take care of some unfinished business."

She could tell that her words disappointed Dawn, but this was something she had to do.

"You'll come with me when you're finished with your business?" Dawn asked.

Lynn saw the need in Dawn's eyes and realized she wasn't the only one who had hungered for family.

"And you have my phone number."

Lynn nodded.

"Then I'm going to head out and take care of some business of my own. This room is rented for the next couple of days. You should be safe here as long as you don't venture out where somebody could recognize you. I'm just a phone call away, Lynn."

Lynn stood and walked her sister to the door. "I still

can't believe everything that's happened, everything you've told me."

"I know, but trust me, it's all real."

"A couple of days, that's all I need," Lynn replied.

The two embraced, and then Dawn was gone, leaving Lynn alone with her thoughts in the silence of the motel room.

She sank down on the edge of one of the two beds. For all intents and purposes, she'd lost her past. Everything she'd believed in had been stripped away from her.

Jonas had wanted her because he'd known about the gene enhancement. He'd masterminded her kidnapping because he'd wanted a superbaby he could raise into a superthief. And he'd succeeded. Oh, how he had succeeded.

She'd been trained by the best that money could buy, her abilities had been honed to perfection, and she'd used them for Jonas.

What would her life have been like if Dunst hadn't kidnapped her? She'd have been raised with Dawn, in a lab, she supposed. Would Rainy Carrington have eventually found her? Would she have been reunited with the woman who'd given her life? She would never know the answer to these particular questions. She would only know the sadness of what might have been.

Her past was disintegrating into the dust of lies, but her future loomed ahead, a future she now controlled.

But she couldn't go forward with that future until she cleaned up what was left of her past.

Where to begin that job? Nick. She had to deal with him. Even though her heart rebelled at the thought of having anything more to do with him, she knew he was her ticket to cleaning up the mess she was in.

With this thought in mind, she went to the phone and dialed in his cell phone number. He answered on the second ring.

"Nick. It's me."

"Lynn, where are you? Do you have any idea how much trouble you're in now? How in the hell did you manage to rig explosives at the station?" His voice held a strained intensity.

"None of that is important now. I need to talk to you."

"Then turn yourself in," he replied. "We'll sort things out here."

"No. I'm not coming in there." She couldn't be in control if they were at the police station, and Lynn would never again place herself in a spot where she wasn't in control.

She frowned thoughtfully. "Does that cottage of yours have a telephone?"

"Yes…why?"

"Be there in half an hour and I'll call you there and tell you where I'll meet you." She could tell he didn't like the plan, that he'd much prefer she turn herself in and go through the appropriate channels. But he acquiesced. She carefully memorized the number he gave her to the phone at his beachfront hideaway, then disconnected the call.

The last time she'd been at that cottage she'd had no idea that Nick was an FBI agent. She'd only known him as the man who excited her, fascinated her, drew her like none other.

It was just after eleven when the cab Lynn rode in let her out several blocks from the road that led to Nick's cottage.

Seeing him again would be difficult. The taste of his betrayal still lingered in her mouth, still burned in her heart. There was a part of her that desperately wanted to believe what he'd said to her, that getting close to her had begun as a job but had become something far more. But she was afraid to believe in anything at this moment.

She crept up on the cottage, checking the area to make certain Nick hadn't arranged some sort of trap for her. She'd told him she'd call to set up a meeting with him, hoping that she would catch him here alone.

There was no indication that a trap had been set. Nick's car was in the driveway, and the night was silent except for the distant roar of waves to shore. The briny scent of the salt water was thick in the humidity of the night, and she remembered that night when she had Nick had walked on the beach at Smokey's. She hardened her heart against those memories.

She sneaked up to the porch and peered into the front window. Although a lamp was on, nobody was in the living room. Soundlessly she went around the cottage, peeking into windows to make certain there weren't agents waiting to pounce out and slap handcuffs on her.

Each room that she looked into appeared empty, except the kitchen. There she saw Nick seated at the table, the telephone at his elbow.

For a long moment she merely looked at him through the window, drinking in the masculine features that had become so familiar to her over the past couple of weeks.

He looked tired and worried and yet still so handsome that her heartache grew in intensity. She drew in a deep breath, refusing to become an emotional mess. She had things to take care of, and Nick could help her straighten them out.

She knocked on the kitchen window. His gaze shot to her, surprise lifting his dark brows. He got up from the table and unlocked the back door to let her in.

For a moment neither of them said anything. The past twenty-four hours and everything that had happened in that time hung between them along with a barrier of distrust.

"I thought you were going to call and arrange a meeting place," he finally said to break the silence.

"I didn't want to give you a chance to have a bunch

of men there to arrest me." She pulled out a chair and sat at the table. "I want to deal."

She hoped they could keep this on a purely professional level and not discuss or delve into anything personal that had happened between the two of them.

"There's only one thing you have to deal with," he replied, and sat across from her at the table.

She nodded. "I know…Jonas."

"And you're willing to give him up to us?"

There was a part of her that wanted to tell him no, a part of her that yearned to hold on to the fantasy of Jonas's goodness and love. But that was a child's desire, and over the past twenty-four hours Lynn had been thrust into an adulthood where there was no space for childish whims and hanging on to what had never been.

Had she been a beloved goddaughter to Jonas, or just an asset he'd stolen, a tool to be used? Things would be easier to understand if she could believe that, but the situation wasn't so black and white. Yes, Jonas had used her, molded her into his own personal thief, but that didn't mean he didn't also care about her. He'd given her everything she could need growing up. And deep in her heart, she still loved him—which made what she was about to do horribly difficult.

"Since I called you, I've given this a lot of thought," she began slowly. "I met with Richard Dunst and I now know that Jonas is someplace here in the city. He's preparing to fly out of the country as soon as he hears from me."

Nick's jaw muscles tightened. "If he gets out of the country, we'll probably never catch him." He gazed at her for a long moment.

She held his gaze, refusing to look away. "I have a number to reach him and I can set up a meeting. You and your men can be there to arrest him. But before I do that, I have to know that my name will be cleared, just like we discussed before."

"What if he doesn't agree to meet you?" he asked.

"Oh, he will." She looked away from Nick and instead focused her gaze out the back door where the deepest night shadows hung heavy.

She sighed, a touch of thick emotion creeping up her throat. "I always thought of myself as Rapunzel, a princess so beloved that her godfather kept her locked up and protected from the world." Her heart swelled with grief as she mourned all that she'd lost, all that she now knew had never been. "Now I realize I wasn't like Rapunzel at all. I was the golden goose, kept in a cage until it was time to produce more wealth."

"Lynnette." His voice was so soft she wanted to fall into it, let it carry her away to a place where there wasn't so much pain.

Instead she drew a deep breath and looked at him once again. "Trust me. He'll meet me. He'll want a

chance to talk me into going with him. He won't want
to lose his golden goose."

"I'm sorry, Lynn." He reached across the table, but
stopped when his hand was mere inches from hers. "I
know you loved him and I can only imagine what must
be going through your head, through your heart right
now."

She suddenly remembered him telling her that
there were some people who shouldn't be parents,
that there were people who didn't make the best of
parents. She'd thought he'd been talking about his
own situation at the time. Now she realized he might
have been warning her about what lay ahead.

"Tell me something, Nick, were the things you told
me about your family true, or was that something
made up to get closer to me?"

His hand that had been close but not touching hers,
touched her then. Just a light touch to the back of her
hand, but it was a touch that sent a wave of emotion
through her. "I never lied to you, Lynnette. Everything
I said to you was always the truth. I'm guilty of not
telling you everything, but what I did tell you was always the truth."

She moved her hand away from his. She couldn't
stand his touch, because she wanted it so badly, because
it reminded her of all she'd believed they'd shared.
"Did you go see your father? Were fences mended?"
she asked.

His eyes, already such a dark brown, deepened in hue to almost black. At the same time a furrow formed in the center of his forehead as he frowned. "No, fences weren't mended. My father wanted to tell me one last time what a disappointment I was, that he would curse me with his dying breath. It was one more kick in my face after too many years of kicks."

Even though she still harbored bitterness in her heart toward Nick and she wanted to maintain that anger to keep the pain at bay, she couldn't help but be touched by his words.

"I'm sorry, Nick."

"Don't be." He shook his head. "I made peace with my family and my choices a long time ago. I hoped that you'd never have to face the same kind of thing, but here we are."

Lynn reached into her pocket and pulled out the slip of paper that had Jonas's phone number on it. She placed it on the table between them. "And now it's time I make peace, as well. I'll set up a meeting for sometime in the morning."

"Where?"

She frowned thoughtfully. "He'll never return to the mansion so it can't be there. What about here? I can even tell him the truth, that it's a place you own and that sometime last week you gave me the key. There would be no reason for him to be suspicious about this place."

Nick leaned back in his chair, obviously contemplating her suggestion. "I guess this would be as good a place as anywhere. At least here we don't have to worry about civilians getting in the way." He nodded. "Yeah, we can make it work here if he agrees to show up."

"He'll agree, and if he doesn't I can make certain he'll agree to meet me before he leaves the country."

"How can you do that?" Nick asked curiously.

"If you can get me into the mansion and to Jonas's computer, then I can freeze all of his banking accounts."

"We've already done that," Nick replied. "I had them frozen about an hour ago."

"You might think you froze all of Jonas's accounts, but I'm sure he has accounts you don't know about. He has accounts in banks all over the world, in places there would be no records of here."

"Then we'll get you to that computer to freeze the rest of them. Even if he agrees to meet with you, I'd like to make sure he can't get to his accounts."

She reached for the phone, surprised to see her fingers trembling slightly. Before she grabbed the receiver she paused and looked at Nick once again. "Even though I have absolutely no reason to trust you, I am trusting that you aren't lying to me, that all charges against me will be dropped and I can walk away from all this unscathed."

"I swear," he said solemnly.

She had to believe him. She picked up the receiver and dialed the number Dunst had given her. Jonas answered it on the second ring.

"Uncle Jonas," she said.

"Lynn, baby, where are you? Why didn't you come with Richard to meet me? I've been anxiously waiting for you from the minute I heard about your escape."

"I needed to think, Uncle Jonas. I'm so confused by everything. I was so scared in jail."

"I know, honey. I'm sorry you had to go through that all alone." There was a long pause. "Lynn, baby, I tried desperately to get you out of there, but I've been betrayed by our government contact."

"Yes, Richard told me," she replied. "But how? What happened?"

"I can't tell you how upset I am. I've been handing over to him the precious things you've been retrieving, but he's been selling them, Lynn. He's as crooked as they come and now he's trying to destroy me. He has position and power and he will make things difficult for us."

Lynn listened dispassionately, surprised to discover that she was already moving away from Jonas, that the seedling of strength she'd felt growing over the past couple of days had bloomed. She could give him up and she could walk away.

"Lynn, it's vital we go away. This contact, he won't stop until he sees us both in jail. While you were in police custody…you didn't say anything about our work, did you?"

"I refused to speak to any of the officers who tried to talk to me," she replied, repeating what she'd told Dunst.

"Good, good. We can continue our work elsewhere…in another country."

Bitterness swelled up inside her at his words. It was just as she'd thought. He didn't want her, but he needed her. He needed her unique skills, her unusual abilities, to carry out his own plots and pillaging.

"I want to see you," she said. "I need some time to think. I'm exhausted, Uncle Jonas. Can we wait until morning to leave? Can we meet in the morning someplace and talk? Please, Uncle Jonas."

There was a long silence and she knew he was probably irritated by her request. "Lynn, there's nothing to be confused about. We need to leave here. Time is of the essence."

"I got the urn, Uncle Jonas. I managed to get it and hide it before the FBI took me down. I wanted to surprise you with it." It was bait she hoped he'd swallow. "I don't want to leave it behind. I need tonight to get it from where I hid it. I have to be careful because the police are looking for me."

There was another long moment of silence, and Lynn knew Jonas was weighing his options. The urn and vase were priceless, but so was his freedom.

"All right, I'll meet you in the morning," he finally said as greed ultimately won out. "Meet me at the airport. I have the plane ready to go."

"We can't meet there. My face is being splashed all over the news and I'm sure the authorities will be watching the airports. If you're seen with me, you may be arrested as on accessory." She hesitated, then continued. "I know just the place where it will be safe for both of us," she continued. "You know I've been seeing Nick for the last couple of weeks." Once again her gaze went to Nick. "He's got a little cottage on Harbor Road. A couple of nights ago he made me dinner there and gave me the key to the place. We can meet there. He won't even know about it."

She gripped the phone tightly and looked away from Nick as memories of that night cascaded through her mind. They had nearly made love that night. She almost wished they had, that she'd have that memory to carry with her despite the knowledge that he'd used her.

"You're sure it will be safe?" he asked.

"Why wouldn't it?" she countered. "Nick told me nobody knows he stays there, that it's just a little weekend getaway he keeps. It should be perfect for us."

"All right. Ten o'clock," Jonas said. "I'll meet you there at ten. We'll only have a few minutes, Lynn, then we must board the plane and leave. Richard will have the plane ready for us. I hope, I pray you'll come with me, Lynn. I can't imagine you not being with me."

"I'll talk to you in the morning," she replied. "Uncle Jonas, I love you." She disconnected the call before he could reply, before he could tell her that he loved her, too.

"Ten o'clock in the morning," she said.

Nick stood. "I'll set things up on my end, then we'll get you to the house to freeze the rest of Jonas's assets."

While Nick got on his cell phone and made the arrangements he needed to make, Lynn slipped out the back door and stood on the small patio, staring out to where the moon played on the water.

She was betraying the man who had raised her and it weighed heavily on her heart. She thought of all the times she'd eagerly waited for Jonas to return home from his trips. How happy she'd been when he'd given her an assignment to retrieve a treasure. She'd been so sure she was doing good, pleasing Jonas and helping her country.

Instead she'd been nothing more than a common criminal, a highly trained burglar, the almost perfect thief. She'd used her computer skills to crack into security files. She'd used her physical skills to steal, all because she loved Jonas.

Jonas wasn't the good man she'd believed him to be. The crimes he was suspected of weren't just crimes of property; they were crimes of people. He belonged behind bars.

Nick stepped out the door. "Are you all right?" She hesitated, then nodded.

"I'm fine. This is just a bit difficult."

He came to stand just behind her. She could smell his nearness and feel his body heat. "I know it's difficult, Lynnette." Again his voice was soft and filled with empathy. "But, it has to be done. I can't begin to tell you the kinds of things that Jonas has done to hurt people. And I hate it that he's hurt you."

"I know." She sensed that he was about to touch her, and she turned to face him and stepped aside, not wanting his touch, afraid that it would make her shatter into a million pieces.

He shoved his hands in his jeans pockets, his eyes dark and enigmatic. "You ready to go to the house and freeze the rest of his accounts?"

"I'm ready," she said softly.

She knew it would be her last time in the house where she'd been raised. She knew that tonight she was closing the book of her past to open the book of an uncertain future.

Chapter 13

It was after two when they returned to the cottage. Lynn had stayed true to her word. She'd changed the passwords for the last of Jonas's bank accounts, making it impossible for him to access any of them, then she had packed two suitcases of clothing and personal items and had left the mansion for the last time.

She hadn't asked Nick to take her back to the motel. She hadn't wanted to be alone. Being in the house again had been difficult. Knowing that she'd never again return had been nearly devastating.

While Nick waited downstairs with several other agents who were watching the house, Lynn had sat in her bedroom and cried silent tears of grief. The very fabric of her life had been ripped out from beneath her, and she mourned for the man she'd thought her godfather had been.

Godfather. Even that had been a lie. He hadn't been good friends with her parents, he hadn't adopted her through legal channels. He'd stolen her.

When she finally left the bedroom, her tears were spent, and she knew they were the last she'd ever shed for Jonas White.

She'd said painful goodbyes to Rita and Arturo, who were confused and frightened by the FBI who had the house staked out. The elderly Cuban couple were planning on staying with one of their sons and looking for new work. They were good, hard workers and Lynn felt confident they would have no problem being hired by somebody.

Rita had hugged her tight and sobbed and Lynn had silently cursed the man who had caused all this pain, the man who had betrayed all their love. She promised to keep in touch with the couple who had been like surrogate parents to her.

When they finally returned to the cottage, Nick finalized his plans for the morning meeting with his team, and she returned to the patio, once again looking out to the ocean.

When she'd been at the house she'd grabbed her cell phone and she now used it to call Dawn and arrange to meet her at the motel room around noon the next day. By then Jonas would be in custody and there was nothing else keeping Lynn here. She would be on to her new life and new challenges.

Arrangements made, she put the cell phone in her pocket and stared out at the waves. Always before when she'd gazed at the water she'd thought of the parents she believed had been lost in a storm. She'd mourned the parents she couldn't remember and had wondered how her life would have been different if they hadn't taken their yacht out on that fateful day.

Now she knew the truth—that there had been no eccentric couple who had drowned in a boating accident. Jonas had lied. Now she knew why her Internet search had yielded no results about the tragic boating accident. It had been a figment of Jonas's manipulation and evil mind. He'd even manufactured photos and news clippings to satisfy the questions he'd known she would ask.

However, there was Dawn. The empty spaces in her heart filled with warmth as she embraced the reality of a sister. She and Dawn shared the same genetic makeup.

She leaned against the railing around the patio and stared at the moon overhead. She thought of a woman named Lorraine Carrington, Rainy, her mother. What exactly had happened to Rainy? Had she discovered what had been done to her, and had that been the reason for her murder?

She hadn't asked Dawn who their father was. If she and Dawn had come from eggs from Rainy, then who had fertilized those eggs? There might be a man out there somewhere who was her biological father.

She wanted answers. She wanted to learn more about the woman who had been her mother and the friends who had held her dear.

She turned and looked through the window where Nick sat at the table. His thick, dark hair was tousled as if he'd run his hands through it more than once in the last few minutes. His features were animated as he talked on the phone.

She didn't want to leave here without making love to him. The realization hit her like a bolt of lightning.

It didn't matter that he'd betrayed and used her. It didn't matter that she would be leaving soon to explore the secrets of her own life.

What did matter was that, even knowing all this, she still wanted Nick. It was the one thing that was clear in her head, and the idea of being held in his arms and loved to the fullest extent both excited her and filled her with awe.

She turned back around and once again stared up at the moon. Beginning tomorrow she would be on a journey that would take her far away from Miami and everything she knew.

She should be afraid but she wasn't. The inner

strength she'd discovered she possessed filled her up, and in that strength she knew her own desire.

She heard the sound of the back door opening and closing, but didn't turn.

Nick walked to her side, bringing with him the masculine scent of his that filled her head. "Are you all right?" he asked softly.

She nodded. "I'm fine. You seem to be asking me that a lot."

"I know how difficult this must be for you."

She finally turned to look at him. His dark brown eyes glittered in the moonlight. "It's not as difficult as I thought it would be. If even half of what you've shown me is true, Jonas deserves to go to jail for the rest of his life."

Nick leaned on the railing and looked up at the moon. "I was thirteen when I recognized that my father was a monster. I watched him beat a man almost to death. I knew at that moment that my only hope for a good future was to get away from him and I knew I wanted to choose a path opposite from the path he'd chosen."

She memorized his features in her mind—the strong lines of his jaw, the slightly square chin, the rugged planes that somehow came together in a face both handsome and filled with strength and character. "So you became an FBI agent, fighting evil with good," she said lightly, fighting her desire to lean against him.

"Something like that." He looked at her once again, his gaze soft. "Lynnette, I meant what I said to you before you escaped from the police station. I never, ever meant to hurt you."

"But it was your job to bring Jonas down, and I was a tool for you to use to do that," she said, unable to help the touch of hurt that colored her tone.

He nodded slowly. "We'd worked so hard for so long to get to Jonas, and my supervisor was getting impatient. It was his idea to try to get at Jonas through you, and I agreed to it. I thought it was going to be easy."

He reached up and gently swiped a strand of her hair away from her face. The gesture was achingly familiar, and a swell of desire swept through her. "But that night at Smokey's when I held you in my arms, I realized this was going to be the most difficult assignment I'd ever accomplished. I wanted you, and it had nothing to do with my job or getting to Jonas, nothing to do with my supervisor telling me to get close to you. I wanted you for myself."

She'd wanted to hear these words from him. She'd needed to know that what they'd shared had been real and not manufactured. "I want you, Nick. I want you to take me to bed and make love to me."

He seemed to freeze in position, his gaze locked with hers. "Lynn, this has been a confusing time for you."

"Wanting you is the one thing I'm not confused about. You don't want me anymore?" She held her breath, wondering if he'd lied about his feelings.

His eyes flashed darkly. "You have no idea how much I want you."

Her breath released itself on a relieved sigh. "Then show me, Nick. I don't need any promises from you. I don't need any tomorrows. I don't need anything but this moment in time. Show me that you want me."

He didn't wait for her to ask him again, but rather grabbed her in an embrace at the same time his mouth crashed down to hers.

He couldn't manufacture the fire in his kiss, the hunger that marked the way he pulled her tightly against him. There was no lie in his arousal, hard against her as she molded her body to his.

When he finally tore his mouth from hers, he gazed at her with desire shining from the dark depths of his eyes. "I don't want to be somebody else who manipulates or uses you." A deep huskiness filled his voice. "This can't be about what I want. It has to be about what you want."

"You can't manipulate or use me, nobody can, ever again," she replied with certitude. "But I know what I want, Nick, and more than anything right now I want to make love with you."

Without saying another word he took her by the hand and led her back into the house. They went through the kitchen and living room and into his bedroom, where the only light was the soft moon rays drifting into the window.

He released her hand when they stood in front of his bed.

"No means no, Lynn. If you change your mind or have any doubts about this, all you have to do is tell me no and we'll stop."

If she'd wanted him before it was nothing like the passion that swept through her now. In reply she moved to the head of the bed and pulled down the bedspread and top sheet. She then turned to face him and pulled her T-shirt over her head.

Nothing else in her life was for certain except the very rightness of this tonight. She hadn't lied to him before when she'd told him she needed no promises from him. She didn't need the promise of a future. She just needed him now.

Once again he seemed frozen. Only his chest moved, rising and falling in accelerated breaths. His hungry gaze never left her as she reached behind and unfastened her bra.

The wispy garment fell to the floor as she kicked off her shoes at the same time.

The only thing he moved was his gaze as he watched her undress for him. Her bare skin warmed with a flush, and her fingers trembled slightly as she lowered her hands to the fastening of her jeans.

The sound of the zipper seemed unnaturally loud in the silence of the room, and the fabric rubbed her sensitive skin as she slid the jeans down her thighs. It wasn't nerves or fear that made her tremble and flush, it was sweet anticipation.

It was only when she pulled her panties off that the inertia that had gripped him snapped. As she slid into bed beneath the sheet, he yanked his clothes off in a frenzy.

His shirt fell to the floor, exposing his beautiful, tautly muscled chest. He kicked off his shoes and pulled off his socks, then tore off his jeans in a near frenzy of motion. It was as if he was afraid if he didn't hurry she might change her mind. But she wouldn't. She knew this was what she wanted.

When he was naked, he slipped into bed and pulled her into his arms at the same time his mouth found hers. His body was warm against hers as he deepened the kiss with his tongue.

She moved against him, loving the sensation of his firm hairy chest against her taut nipples. A deep ache gnawed in the pit of her stomach, an ache that spoke of hungry need.

She gasped as his hands cupped her breasts, his thumbs raking over the peaks and shooting shivers of delight through her. His mouth left her lips and trailed down her throat, across her collarbones, then to one of her nipples.

Her hands clutched in his hair as his tongue caressed first the tip of one breast then the other. A building tension twisted inside her as her pleasure grew.

She moaned as his hands moved down her body. He splayed them over the flat of her stomach, then raked them down the sides of her hips. Once again his mouth sought hers in a kiss that swept all other conscious thought away.

"Lynn...sweet Lynn," he murmured as his hands brushed her inner thigh. Her hips arched toward his touch, wanting the intimacy of his hands on her where no other man's hands had ever been.

Still his fingers caressed the sensitive skin of her inner thighs. The soft, featherlike strokes electrified her as he teased and tormented her by not touching her where she wanted him most.

She moved her hands down his body. She tangled her fingers in his chest hair, then moved them down across his muscular abdomen.

A moan escaped him as her fingers moved over his hips. Before she could explore his body further, he touched her at her center and she cried out his name.

His finger rubbed against her and it was as if every nerve in her body began and ended where he touched. Her entire body quivered. She moved her hips in a wild rhythm against him as the tension inside her built.

She was on fire, burning in flames of Nick. When she thought she could stand no more, when the tension inside her threatened to overwhelm her, it shattered and crashed through her, sending rivulets of warmth through her veins.

She was breathless and gasping but still not sated. She wanted more. "Nick…please…" She reached down and encircled his hard length with her hand. She liked the feel of him, hard and yet smooth and velvety.

"Lynnette." He groaned her name and at the same time rolled away from her. He reached into the night-stand and pulled out a small foil package.

A condom. Relief flooded through her. She hadn't even thought about safe sex. Thank goodness one of them had their wits about them.

He ripped open the package and rolled the condom on himself and when he hovered over the top of her she opened her legs to welcome him.

For a long moment he gazed down at her, and in his eyes she saw not only desire, not only want, but also a gentleness that spoke of something more.

She closed her eyes, not wanting to see that, knowing that if she saw that he truly cared about her it would only make leaving that much more difficult.

She gripped his hips and pulled him closer, letting him know she was ready. She tensed as he began to enter her. She expected pain, but there was none, just a bit of discomfort that lasted only a moment.

He lay perfectly still against her, not moving a muscle. "Are you all right?" he whispered against her ear. "Am I hurting you?"

"Yes…I mean no, you aren't hurting me."

Then he moved and she gasped as pleasure swept through her.

Her senses were alive with him…his familiar masculine scent, the play of his back muscles beneath her fingertips, the sound of his heartbeat and rapid breathing. He filled her up on all levels.

She'd listened to her friends talk about sex, but nothing they had said had prepared her for the emotional rush. She'd expected physical pleasure, but she hadn't expected the intimacy that transcended the physical act.

She'd wanted him to make love to her, but she hadn't expected her heart to be involved. But it was. Her heart swelled with emotion as she felt him deep inside her.

As he moved his hips against hers and their heartbeats crashed in rhythm, she felt as if he surrounded her, invaded her in body and soul.

It was an invasion she welcomed. She wrapped her legs around his and ran her hands down the smooth warm skin of his back as he sent that crazy, wonderful tension building inside her once again.

He crashed his lips onto hers as their hips thrust together frantically. Tongues battled as they kissed with a hunger that was all consuming.

"Lynnette," he moaned when he tore his lips from hers and instead trailed them down the curve of her jaw.

She loved it that he'd called her by her real name and not the diminutive. Nobody else in her life called her Lynnette.

That was her last conscious thought as physical sensation swept away everything else. Faster and faster they moved in unison and she was swept higher and higher on a plane of pleasure.

She tumbled over the precipice, moaning his name, and at the same time he stiffened against her, a groan escaping his lips.

For a long moment they remained locked together, waiting for heartbeats to slow, for breath to return. Her hand stroked down his back, loving the feel of his warm skin. Nick. They said you always remember your first lover. She had a feeling she would have remembered him even if he hadn't been her first.

He finally raised himself up and looked down at her, his gaze holding a wealth of tenderness. "You okay?" He gently moved a strand of her hair away from her eyes. "I didn't hurt you, did I?"

Yes, he'd hurt her when she'd realized he'd used her. He'd hurt her in those moments when she'd seen him at the Markam Convention Center and realized he'd betrayed her. That's what she wanted to tell him, but instead she shook her head to assure him he had not hurt her. Knowing now what she did about Jonas, she couldn't fault him for what he had done. She couldn't hold on to her bitterness where he was concerned.

He eased away from her. "I'll be right back." He slid from the bed and disappeared into the bathroom.

Lynn rolled over on her side and stared toward the window where the moonlight filtered in through the sheer curtains. Her body tingled with the warmth of their lovemaking, and she had no regrets about what they had shared. She was glad it had been Nick who had introduced her to the pleasure of lovemaking.

He returned to the bed and gathered her in his arms. She snuggled against him although she knew she should get up and go back to her motel.

"What are you thinking?" he asked, his voice a soft whisper in the darkness as he tightened his arms around her.

"That I'm glad we made love, that I'm glad we had this night together because tomorrow I'm leaving."

"Leaving? What do you mean?" He leaned away and gazed down at her.

"As soon as you and your men arrest Jonas, I'm leaving Miami."

"Why? Lynn, there's no reason you can't build a life here. With your computer skills you could find a job easily."

"I found out I have a sister."

"What? Where?" He reached out and turned on the bedside lamp.

She sat up as she realized she wanted to talk about it. She wanted to tell him some of the secrets that Jonas had wanted her to keep to herself. "In the last twenty-four hours I've discovered some things about my past, about where I came from. There never were eccentric millionaires who were my parents and who were lost at sea. That was just another of Jonas's lies."

He looked at her in surprise. "So how did he get you as a baby?"

Lynn told him about being kidnapped as a baby and that her biological mother was dead. She didn't tell him that Dawn was responsible for her escape from the police station. She certainly didn't want to cause Dawn any problems.

"I guess Jonas wanted a baby he could raise and train to do his dirty work," she said.

His dark eyes were filled with speculation. "Lynn, I know now you pulled off a lot of robberies for Jonas. I also know that the men who tried to catch you said you were like a superhuman phantom, able to accomplish physical feats that were nearly impossible."

"I was well trained," she replied, but she was unable to hold his gaze.

"Well trained," he repeated flatly. "You know, I saw signs of your unusual quickness that night at Sensations when you defended yourself against that drunk. It was more than mere training that I saw. You have amazing abilities. Talk to me. You can tell me. You can trust me, Lynn."

"I do have some unusual abilities," she finally agreed.

He touched her cheek. "And you aren't telling me everything, are you?"

She looked at him once again. "No, I'm not. But I can't, Nick. I don't have all the answers yet." She was suddenly exhausted. She hadn't expected the emotions that flooded through her as she gazed at him, as she thought about leaving both him and Miami behind. "Maybe we should get some sleep," she finally said. "It's late and tomorrow is going to be a difficult day."

He looked as if he wanted to say something more, but instead he turned off the light and once again gathered her in his arms.

As she molded herself against his warmth in the darkness of the room, she realized that by making love to her, he'd not only won back her trust, he'd also won her heart.

But she'd told him she wanted nothing more from him than this night. She'd insisted she needed no promises, no tomorrows, and he hadn't offered any.

Chapter 14

She awakened just after dawn to find herself alone in the bed. She rolled over on her back and stared up at the ceiling. It was betrayal day.

Today she would betray the man who had raised her, the man who had fed her and clothed her for all her life, the man who had seen to it that she had the best education, the best of everything.

Today she would betray the man who had given her everything but the truth, the man who had kidnapped her and used her to further his own criminal activities.

She was surprised to discover that she felt little regret over what she was going to do. She only hoped when they put Jonas behind bars that Richard Dunst would share the same quarters.

This wasn't just the day she'd betray Jonas, it was also the day she would say goodbye to Miami and follow Dawn to an unknown place to discover the mysteries of the past.

Today was also the day she would say goodbye to Nick.

Nick. Her body still felt the memory of his sensual touch, his demanding kisses. Her heart still felt the wonder and magic of their lovemaking.

It would have been easy to say goodbye to him if she still felt betrayed by him, if she still tasted the acrid flavor of bitterness where he was concerned. But her anger had left, taking with it any bitterness that might linger behind.

The scent of fresh-brewed coffee wafted in the air, and she pulled herself out of bed, grabbed clean clothes from her suitcase and headed for the bathroom and a shower.

As she stood beneath the hot spray of water, she remembered each and every moment of their lovemaking the night before. She would never forget last night.

Nick had made her body sing with his heated caresses and fiery kisses, but he'd also made her heart sing with his tenderness and caring. Saying goodbye to him was going to be more difficult than she'd thought.

Minutes later she entered the kitchen to find him at the table. "Good morning," she said.

He smiled. "Good morning to you. Coffee is ready. I left a cup on the counter for you."

"Thanks." She walked over to the counter and poured herself coffee, then carried the cup to the table and sat down across from him.

"You ready for today?"

She nodded. "As ready as I'm going to get." She took a sip of her coffee, then continued. "I don't have any regrets about setting up Jonas."

"And no regrets about anything else?" His dark eyes held her gaze.

Her cheeks warmed, but she held his gaze. "No, Nick. No regrets at all." She took another sip of her coffee. "Even though I was angry with you, hurt by the fact that I thought you'd used me, I wanted last night with you."

"Are you still angry and hurt?" His expression told her that her answer was important to him.

She hesitated a long moment before answering. "Maybe a little hurt, but you've made me believe that using me was difficult for you, that it was something you had to do. You've made me believe that what I thought we had when we were together was real."

This is what she truly believed, what she desperately wanted to believe, yet she also knew it was possible he was still using her. Until Jonas was in his custody, she was useful to Nick and she couldn't forget that fact.

"It was real, Lynn," he said. "It is very real."

She sat back in her chair. "What's important now is that we get Jonas."

"That's important," he agreed. "But it isn't all that's important. I want you to understand what the last couple of weeks with you have meant to me."

She held up a hand to still whatever more he would say. She didn't want to hear this, not now, not with goodbye so very near.

He looked as if he wanted to say something more, but at that moment a knock tapped at the back door. Nick's team had arrived and the time for personal talk was over.

There was a total of five men who would be responsible for arresting Jonas. They had arrived early to be in place for the meeting between Lynn and her godfather.

Even though it was a little more than three hours before the ten-o'clock meeting, the men each took a post inside the house to wait. Two were stationed on the outside of the house, hidden on the property next door. The other three took positions in each of the two bedrooms and one in the bathroom.

Nick moved his car down the road so it wouldn't be in the driveway to spook Jonas, then he and Lynn sat at the table, listening to the clock tick by the minutes.

"When he gets here, I'll stay out of sight," Nick said. "As soon as he gets into the living room we'll move in to take him down."

"I want an opportunity to speak with him," Lynn said. She needed to tell him that she knew how he'd used her all her life. She needed to look into his eyes and see if there was any love, any affection at all for her.

"I can't make any promises, Lynn. We'll have to see how things go down. At the very least, once we have him in handcuffs, I don't see why you can't have a word or two with him."

Handcuffs. It was almost impossible for her to imagine Jonas in handcuffs. She remembered the bite of the cuffs around her own wrists, and her heart hardened.

It had been Jonas who had placed her in a position to be arrested and handcuffed. It had been his lies that had prompted her to steal and ultimately be caught. She would weep no tears for his arrest.

As the minutes ticked by, she felt a growing tension inside her. What if he didn't show up? What if he'd already left the country? She tried to tell herself he wouldn't leave without the precious urn he thought she had. More important, he wouldn't leave once he found that the passwords on his accounts had been changed and he could no longer access any of his money.

"I wonder if he ever loved me," she said aloud.

Nick knew about whom she was talking. "He probably loves you as much as a man like him is capable of loving." He sighed. "My mother used to tell me that my father loved me despite the fact that he beat me about every other day and ignored me the rest of the time." He smiled, a sad, rueful kind of expression. "I used to think it was a good thing he loved me, because if he didn't I wouldn't have survived him at all."

"It's sad, isn't it, how much we as children need to believe that our families love us, how much we need to believe they would never do anything to hurt us."

"Things could be worse, Lynn," he said. "I could have become just like my father and you could have become just like Jonas."

"Never," she replied fervently. "The only way he got me to steal for him was by lying, by telling me we were accomplishing something good."

She glanced at the clock on the oven. One more hour and everything would be over. She gazed back at Nick. "You know, I felt good when I was stealing those things. I was pleasing Jonas, but I was also pleasing myself. I enjoyed the challenge and I thought I was doing something good."

"Don't beat yourself up, Lynn. You were manipulated by a master."

"I should have known better." She got up from the table and carried her cup to the sink, then turned back to face Nick. "I should have asked more questions, demanded better answers. For the past several months my instincts kept telling me something wasn't right, but I ignored my instincts and instead followed Jonas like a docile lamb."

He got up from the table and walked over to her. He placed his hands on her shoulders, his gaze intense. "Don't blame yourself. It's done. It's over and you're doing the right thing now. He belongs behind bars, and within the next hour or two that's exactly where he'll be."

He pulled her against his chest and willingly she went. She closed her eyes as his arms encircled her. "You're a good person, Lynn," he whispered against her hair. "Don't let him make you question yourself and the kind of person you are. If you do, then he wins."

She nodded, loving him more at this moment than ever before. She knew he was right, but she also knew it would be a long time before her regrets over what she had done for Jonas finally went away.

For a long moment she remained in his embrace, her face turned into the fresh scent of his shirt. She drew in the smell of him, capturing it in her memory for the nights of loneliness she knew lay ahead. She memorized the feel of his hands on her back, those beautiful hands that could be so gentle.

She eased out of his arms and forced a smile to her lips. She had to leave. "This is difficult, you know. Betraying Jonas," she said, focusing on the task at hand. "But I know it's the right thing to do."

Nick's eyes shone with approval. "That's what we all want, Lynn. The world will be a better place if he's not working it."

At nine-thirty Lynn sat in the living room alone, waiting for Jonas's arrival. Nick was in the kitchen. The other men were in place and hidden from sight. All they were missing was the guest of honor.

As she waited, her thoughts went back in time, through her childhood and adolescence. Surely Jonas had loved her just a little? Surely he'd cared about her. But even as she thought this, her mind refused to embrace it.

It was a parent's job to teach their children how to have wings, how to stand on their own, depend on themselves and grow into independent people. That's how people loved their children, by preparing them to leave the nest.

Jonas had done just the opposite. He'd taught her nothing about freedom, had kept her bound to him through fear. He'd wanted to keep her a prisoner forever, using her until she was all used up. That wasn't love.

She heard a car approaching in the distance, and every muscle in her body tensed in anticipation. As the car noise grew louder, Nick stuck his head out the kitchen door and gave her the thumbs-up sign, then disappeared once again.

Lynn stood, heart thumping loudly in her chest. This was it. Her final showdown with Jonas. She went to the front window and looked outside as a black sedan pulled up and parked in the driveway. Jonas got out of the driver's side.

She saw him look around, obviously making sure there was no reason for concern. She stepped to the door and opened it to make sure he could see her.

"Uncle Jonas," she said. She hated even calling him Uncle but knew it was important that she act as if nothing had changed between them. If he sensed anything wrong he'd never come inside, and their plan might fall apart.

He hurried toward the door. "Lynn, thank God." She stepped aside so he could enter the living room. She'd expected Nick's men to move in immediately, but everyone stayed in their hiding places as Jonas hugged her, then stepped back from her.

"It's so good to see you, baby. I was worried sick when I heard that you'd been arrested."

"It was awful." She forced a shudder.

"It's all over now," he replied. "Within hours we'll be safe. Do you have the urn?"

"It's in the bedroom, but before I get it for you I need to know what's going on. Where are we going, Uncle Jonas?"

"So you're coming with me?"

She hesitated a moment, then nodded. "Last night I

wasn't sure. I thought maybe I could stay here in the States, but I realize now I can't. I'm a fugitive from justice," she said. "I can't stay here. I sure don't want to go to prison."

"What did you do to my bank accounts, Lynn?"

"I changed the passwords," she said truthfully. "I didn't want you to leave without me."

"I wouldn't have left without you unless it was absolutely necessary," he replied. "Just because things got screwed up here doesn't mean we can't continue our work someplace else."

Where were Nick and his men? "I'd like that," she said. "And don't worry, I know the new passwords. The accounts are safe."

"Then get the artifacts and let's get out of here," Jonas said. "We've got the jet waiting for us. We can be in Puerto Isla by nightfall."

"I don't think so." Nick stepped into the room from the kitchen, gun in his hand and pointed toward Jonas. "You aren't going anywhere."

"What's this?" Jonas looked from Lynn to Nick, then before she could guess his intent Jonas grabbed her by the hair and pulled her against his chest. She felt the cold steel of a gun barrel at her temple.

Lynn's heart crashed against her rib cage as Nick cursed. "Let her go, Jonas," he said, his features taut. "You don't want to hurt Lynn."

"Of course I don't want to hurt Lynn," Jonas

agreed, his voice smooth as silk. "But I will if necessary. Sorry, baby, but there's no way I'm going to prison. Now, put your gun down, Nick, or I'll shoot her in the head."

Nick's features were tortured, but he bent down and placed his gun on the floor in front of him.

Jonas backed up toward the door as the other three agents stepped into the room from the hallway.

"Hold your fire," Nick exclaimed. "Dammit Jonas, it's over. Let her go."

"You aren't locking me up," he said and tightened his hold around Lynn. "Tell your men to drop their weapons. If you have men outside, you might want to tell them that with my last breath I'll pull this trigger. You'll get me, but she'll be dead. Can you live with that?"

Nick glanced at one of the other men. "Go tell them to hold their fire. Hold their fire, dammit." The agent ran toward the back of the house while the others placed their guns on the floor.

As Jonas half dragged, half carried Lynn out the front door, she felt as if she'd fallen into the middle of a nightmare. The shock of the realization that Jonas would kill her to save himself had her numb.

She hadn't realized until this moment that a small part of her had clung to the belief that Jonas loved her just a little.

They reached the porch, and still the barrel of his

gun drilled into her temple, telling her exactly the extent of his love. He would gladly sacrifice her life to save his own. He would shoot her before he'd allow himself to be taken into custody.

"Hold your fire! Hold your fire!" Nick yelled as he followed them onto the porch.

As Jonas yanked her toward the car, she knew that if he managed to get her inside, then Jonas would get away and the odds of Lynn surviving were minimal.

"I'm sorry, baby," Jonas said. "But you shouldn't have done this. You shouldn't have set me up like this." He opened the driver's-side door, and as he did, Lynn summoned all the strength she'd ever known.

She flung her elbow backward, hitting Jonas's belly. He grunted in surprise and cracked her in the head with the butt of the gun.

She kicked and hit his hand, sending the gun flying from his grip. He shoved her backward and she fell, hitting the ground hard. Before Nick or the agents could do anything to stop him, he was in the car and had started the engine.

Lynn skittered backward like a crab to stop from being run over as Jonas peeled out. The agents fired at the retreating car, but it didn't stop. They ran toward their cars parked down the street, but she knew by the time they managed to give chase Jonas would be gone.

"Call it in," Nick cried as he raced to Lynn's side.

"Are you all right?" He crouched down and grabbed her to his chest.

"He got away," she cried. At the same time she grabbed the side of her head where she'd been hit.

"We'll get him," Nick replied, helping her to her feet. "There's no way he's getting on any plane for Puerto Isla. He'll be in custody in a matter of hours." Although Nick spoke with assurance, she saw the deep frustration burning in his eyes.

"I'm sorry, Nick."

"It's not your fault. We underestimated him. It will never happen again." He took her by the arm. "Come on, let's get you back inside."

Once inside, the first thing Nick did was look at her head where a goose egg had knotted. He wanted to call for the paramedics, but she assured him she was fine. He got an ice pack for her, then got on the phone.

Lynn sat on the sofa and held the pack on her head. She'd known that Jonas was a criminal, and she'd known that he'd used her. But she'd never dreamed that he would have the capacity to kill her.

But he did. She'd felt it in the steadiness of his hand as he'd held the gun to her head. She'd heard it in the even tone of his voice. He'd gambled that Nick wouldn't sacrifice her, and he'd won.

It was fast approaching the noon hour when Nick finally came into the living room and sank down on the sofa next to her. "We lost him."

"Oh, Nick, I'm so sorry. Although I'm not surprised."

He shrugged. "The good thing is his bank accounts are useless to him. We've got men at every airport. Hopefully he'll turn up and we'll be there to arrest him. We have enough on him now to ensure a conviction on a multitude of charges. We'll get him, Lynn. It's just a matter of time. How's your head?"

"Better. You should have taken the chance and shot him."

"I couldn't do that. I couldn't take a chance with your life," he said. He reached for her hand and grabbed it in a tight grip, his eyes as dark as she'd ever seen them. "I've never been more terrified in my life than when I saw that gun pressed to your head."

She pulled her hand from his, a new pain filling her chest as she realized it was time for her to go. "I'm fine. I need to call a cab. I need to get to the Sleepy Time Motel."

He frowned. "You don't need a cab. I'll take you."

"Don't you need to be here, or doing something about Jonas?" she asked.

"It's out of my hands now. We've got agents all over the city looking for him. I can take you wherever you need to go."

In minutes they'd loaded her suitcases in the trunk of his car. For most of the twenty-minute drive to the motel room, they were both quiet.

It was not a comfortable silence. Rather, it was

filled with a tension she'd never felt between them before. She cast a surreptitious glance at Nick. His jaw muscle was knotted, and she wondered what thoughts were whirling in his head.

She was certain he was thinking about Jonas and the escape. After all, he'd worked two long years undercover to see it all fall apart in a matter of minutes. He must be devastated.

She had no words of comfort to offer him, although her heart ached for his disappointment. But that wasn't the only reason her heart ached.

There was no more time to explore the depth of her feelings for Nick. There would be no more times for making love, no more slow dances at Smokey's or walking on the beach and talking about nothing and everything important.

It was time to say goodbye.

When they reached the motel, she saw that Dawn's car wasn't there. Apparently, she hadn't arrived yet. Nick helped Lynn unload her suitcases and carry them inside the room.

"What happens now?" he asked, his gaze dark and brooding as it lingered on her.

"My sister should be arriving soon, then we'll be leaving."

"Are you going to tell me where you're going?"

She thought about it, then shook her head. "To tell the truth, I'm not sure exactly where we're headed."

He stepped close to her, so close she could feel his breath on her face and smell the scent of him. "Secrets. I see them in your eyes." She didn't reply. She didn't know what to say.

All she knew for certain at this moment was that saying goodbye to him was going to be more difficult than she'd thought. Not that he was asking her to stay, she thought. He'd gotten what he needed from her even though Jonas had managed to escape.

And she'd gotten what she needed from him—a glorious night of lovemaking to remember for the rest of her life....

"Lynnette." His voice, soft and deep, pulled her from her thoughts. She looked into his eyes, and what she saw there frightened her more than anything she'd ever faced. "Don't go."

Those two words shot through her heart like twin daggers. She hadn't expected to hear them from him. She hadn't realized until this moment how much she'd wanted to hear them from him.

He placed his hands on her shoulders and drew her closer against him. Her head fit perfectly just beneath his chin. She leaned into him and closed her eyes.

She was capable of doing amazing physical feats, she could hear the wings of a butterfly in the air and endure a man who had a gun to her head, but nothing had prepared her for this.

"Don't leave," he murmured into her hair at the

same time that his arms encircled her. "I've dated a lot of women, have had my share of relationships, but I've never felt about anyone like I feel about you."

It would have been easy if he'd just been using her. She'd hurt when she'd believed that, but it was nothing like the pain that ripped through her now.

"I have to go," she said, and kept her face turned into his chest.

"Why? Tell me your secrets, Lynn."

She finally looked up at him. "I can't, Nick." Reluctantly she pulled away from him and stepped out of his embrace. "I can't tell you why, but I have to leave."

His gaze held hers intently, and he shoved his hands into his pockets. "So this is it? We make love last night and we say goodbye today?"

She felt the pain she saw reflected in his eyes. It shocked her, and she realized his feelings for her were as deep as hers for him. "Nick, there are things I can't tell you about, things I have to do before I can go on with my life."

"Are you in trouble?"

She didn't know how to answer that question. "I'm not sure." She had no idea where the circumstances of her birth and Rainy's death might take her.

He reached out for her hands and squeezed them tightly. "I'm an FBI agent, Lynn. If you're in trouble, talk to me. Let me help."

"I have to do this for myself, Nick. I had to find out about my past before I can go forward with my future."

He squeezed her hands once again. "You're an amazing woman."

She smiled. "Thank you, but I'm just beginning to know the woman I am…to envision the woman I can be." Aware that Dawn would arrive at any moment, she knew she could no longer put off the final goodbye.

"Nick—" she pulled her hands from his "—you need to go now." The words threatened to choke her.

"One more thing before I leave." He reached out and pulled her back into his arms, and his mouth claimed hers in a kiss so deep, so complete, that tears burned her eyes.

When he finally released her, his gaze held a wistfulness she felt in her soul. "Will you be back?" he asked, his voice sounding deeper than usual.

"Maybe when I've taken care of what I need to."

"How long do you think that will be?"

She drew a deep breath. "I don't know. Days… weeks…I just don't know. Nick, I can't think about any kind of a future right now. I don't even know what's going to happen an hour from now."

"I'll wait, you know. However long it takes. We had magic, Lynn. I don't want it to end. All you have to do is tell me there's a reason for me to wait."

She started to open her mouth to reply, but he placed a finger over her lips. "Not now. The past forty-eight hours of your life haven't exactly been calm. You get where you need to go, Lynnette White, then if you want me to wait for you, if you think we can have some kind of future, you call me."

He didn't wait for her reply but slid out the door and into the afternoon sunshine.

She moved to the doorway, the late-July sunshine almost blinding her, bringing tears to her eyes as she watched him get into his car and roar off.

The moment he was gone Dawn pulled up in her car and stuck her head out the window. "Come on, shake a leg, sis. We've got a flight to catch."

With those words, Lynn's future reached out to her, even as she mourned what might have been.

Chapter 15

The next two hours passed in a blur for Lynn. Dawn explained to her that they would be flying into Phoenix, and would rent a car there and continue on to the Athens, Arizona.

They boarded the plane, and she and Dawn made small talk until they were served soft drinks and pretzels by the flight attendant. It was only when the flight attendant left them alone that Lynn began to ask questions.

"Tell me about you," Lynn said. "Where have you been, what's your background?"

"I was raised in the lab by scientists," Dawn began. "I trained at the lab and was educated there except for one year that I spent attending the Athena Academy. I was there my junior year, then went back to the lab to continue my studies and training."

"What's the academy like?" Lynn asked. She wanted something, anything, to keep her mind off her painful goodbye to Nick.

"It's a wonderful place for girls between the seventh and the twelfth grade. It has state-of-the-art training facilities and the best educational programs in the world. Students there not only do the usual studies, but also are trained in martial arts, weaponry, survival courses and at least three languages."

"Why did you only attend for a year?"

"Look, my background isn't important," Dawn said, her eyes flashing more green than gold. There were secrets there, Lynn thought, secrets that Dawn wasn't willing to share. "What's important is finding out the truth about us and about Rainy."

"Tell me about Rainy," Lynn said, eager to learn anything she could about the woman who had been their biological mother.

"From everything I've learned about her, she was a wonderful woman. She was one of the students the first year that Athena Academy opened. She started there when she was thirteen and remained one of the top students in her class until she graduated. But if you really want to find out about what kind of a person Rainy was, you need to talk to the Cassandras."

"The Cassandras?"

Dawn ripped open her bag of pretzels and nodded. "When Rainy was a senior at the Athena Academy, she became the leader of a group of girls who called themselves the Cassandras. They began as schoolmates working as a team, but they became the best of friends. Rainy was going to meet with the Cassandras on the night she died." Dawn popped one of the pretzels into her mouth as Lynn digested all she was learning.

"Did she tell the Cassandras why she wanted to meet with them that night?" she asked.

Dawn shook her head. "All she told them was that she needed them to meet her and Christine Evans, Athena's school principal, at Christine's bungalow on the school grounds. All the Cassandras who could showed up to wait for Rainy. All she'd told Christine was that she wanted to look through the school records, but Christine didn't know what she wanted to look for."

"And Rainy never showed up for the meeting." Lynn was surprised to discover a wave of grief sweeping over her. She'd long ago mourned the death of her imaginary parents, and now she mourned the mother she'd never know.

Dawn reached over and touched Lynn's hand. "I know," she said softly.

Lynn cast her a smile. "It's just sad. In the space of

a sentence I found my mother and lost her." She took a sip of her soda. "Tell me about these other women, the Cassandras."

"There are six of them. Alex Forsythe is a forensic scientist, Josie Lockworth is in the Air Force and is an aeronautical engineer. Tory Patton is…"

"I know her," Lynn interjected. "I mean, not personally, but I've seen her as a reporter on television."

Dawn nodded. "That's right. Then there's Kayla Ryan, who's a police lieutenant. Samanatha St. John works for the CIA and Darcy Steele is a former Hollywood makeup artist and private investigator."

"Wow, an impressive bunch of women," Lynn said. And what was she? Nothing more than an ordinary thief. When this was all over she vowed to make something of herself, to use her talents to become a dynamic and positive influence.

"They're more than impressive because of the jobs they do," Dawn continued. "What's really so special about them is the bond they forged while they were classmates. When these women were at the Athena Academy they made a promise to one another, that if any of them called for help, they would be there for each other. That night Rainy called on the Cassandra Promise."

"Well, what happened when she didn't arrive at the meeting place?"

"Initially it was thought that Rainy's car wreck had just been a tragic accident, but since then investigators have learned otherwise. Alex and Kayla were the main force behind that. Rainy was murdered, and at the time of her death we think she had realized that her eggs had been mined and was pursuing the truth. We think that's what got her killed."

"My head is spinning," Lynn said. "This is all so confusing."

"It's a lot of information," Dawn replied. "And there's so much more to tell you. But maybe we should both try to catch a nap. When we get to Phoenix we've got a short car drive ahead of us, then we're meeting with Kayla. I have a feeling it's going to be a long day."

Dawn punched the button to put her seat back, and Lynn turned her attention out the plane window. Outside was nothing but blue sky, and she felt as if she'd been thrust into a vast sea where nothing was as it should be and what had been was nothing more than a dream.

Had she made a mistake in coming with Dawn? Certainly the stories Dawn had shared with her sounded fantastic, yet they held a ring of truth she couldn't deny. No, this wasn't a mistake. This was her destiny.

It seemed impossible to believe that only last night she'd been in Nick's arms, and that mere hours ago he'd held her in his arms and told her goodbye.

She felt as if a lifetime had passed. She lowered her seat and closed her eyes, knowing that she would need every ounce of her strength to face what lay ahead.

She awakened when the plane began its descent. Dawn was already awake, and she smiled at Lynn. "Feel better?"

Lynn put her seat up straight. "I don't know. I think I've been numb ever since you broke me out of jail."

Once again Dawn touched her hand. "It's going to be all right, Lynn. We're going to make things right."

Looking into her sister's eyes, eyes so like Lynn's own, Lynn felt a surge of strength. Yes, things would be all right. She and Dawn and the Cassandras would get to the bottom of things and make them right.

Dawn had arranged for a car to be waiting for them, and within minutes of arriving in Phoenix, they were leaving it behind, headed for the small town of Athens.

The scenery was like nothing Lynn had seen before...barren and brown and filled with rock formations that looked like alien landscapes.

As they traveled through the desert, they shared with each other bits and pieces of their former lives.

Lynn found herself telling Dawn about life with Jonas, about the loneliness and isolation of that life and about the nights she'd gone to retrieve precious treasures, believing she was doing something good.

"I know you're unusually fast and agile," Dawn said. "Are there any other enhanced traits?"

"Nothing like your healing ability," Lynn replied. It still amazed her, remembering that moment when Dawn had cut her wrist and the wound had healed before her eyes. "I have enhanced senses. Smell, touch, hearing and sight—they're all unnaturally heightened."

"That must be awful," Dawn exclaimed.

Lynn was surprised by Dawn's reaction and pleased that her sister obviously understood the ramifications of such a gift.

"It can be awful," she agreed. "If I allow myself, I hear a cacophony of sound that hurts my head. I can smell every product anybody has used on their body, what they had for lunch and everything in a mile radius. But I learned fairly early on to block out everything extraneous. The enhanced eyesight isn't bad. It's nice to know I'll probably never need glasses, and the enhanced senses of touch and feel are a real gift."

"How so?"

"When a nice breeze blows across my face, I think I feel it more than other people. The warmth of the sun, the feel of a particular fabric against my skin…" Her voice trailed off as she thought of making love with Nick…the feel of his hands against her skin, the whisper of his breath on her face, on her body. The pleasure had been near mind-blowing. She blushed as she caught Dawn eyeing her curiously.

"I would imagine that means you feel pain more intensely."

Lynn frowned. "I guess. I never really thought about it much before." She reached a hand up to touch the side of her head where Jonas had hit her. It was still tender to the touch, but not bothersome.

She looked at Dawn once again. "If Rainy was our mother, then who is our father?"

"We think he's a man named Thomas King. He's a Navy SEAL commander and his sperm was stolen from a fertility clinic around the time that Rainy's eggs were mined."

"Is he alive?"

"Very much so. I don't know how much you watch the news, but he was held captive for a year in a secret prison on the island of Puerto Isla in Central America."

"Puerto Isla!"

"You know it?"

"I've been there many times. It was one of Jonas's favorite places to visit." Imagine, the last time she'd been there her biological father had been there as well—as a prisoner. "Small world, I guess."

Dawn flashed her a dark look. "Or huge conspiracy."

They fell silent after that. They drove for about an hour leaving behind the Phoenix/Glendale area and arriving in Athens. They drove down Olympus Road, the main street, and Dawn pulled into a motel parking lot.

"Good, Kayla is already here."

Lynn tried to remember which one Kayla was…the six Cassandra women had become jumbled in her mind. "And what does she do?"

"Kayla works as a police lieutenant on the Youngstown, Arizona, police force. Part of her area is Athens."

As they got out of the car nerves jittered through Lynn. With her past burned to ashes, she realized how important it was that these women accept her, like her.

Kayla had been friends with the mother Lynn would never know, and more than anything Lynn wanted Rainy Carrington to be proud of the woman Lynn had become.

A beautiful, tall woman with long brunette hair, brown eyes and a honeyed complexion to envy answered Dawn's knock on room 1. She wrapped her arms around Dawn in a hug and at the same time eyed Lynn in open curiosity over Dawn's shoulder.

"You must be Lynn," she said as she released Dawn. She held a hand out to Lynn. "It's wonderful to meet you. I'm Kayla, and I loved your mother very much."

Together the three of them went into the room, and Kayla motioned them to the small table in the corner of the room. "I'm expecting Darcy at any moment," Kayla said to Dawn. "She called a little while ago and said she had news for us."

While they waited for Darcy to show up, they talked, letting Lynn and Kayla get to know each other.

Lynn learned that Kayla was a single mother. She had a daughter named Jazz who was twelve years old. Jazz was starting Athena Academy in the fall. Kayla explained that she was half Navaho and had grown up on a reservation with loving parents.

Kayla also gave her more information about the other Cassandras and about the woman who was Lynn's surrogate mother, Cleo Patra. Lynn learned that Cleo was a beautiful African American.

"Years ago she was a prostitute in Phoenix," Kayla explained. "She answered a newspaper ad about becoming a surrogate and was placed in the care of Dr. Henry Reagan and Betsy Stone, who was also the nurse for Athena Academy. Cleo's been frightened for a long time by what happened the night the baby was stolen from her, but now she's helping us get to the bottom of all this."

"I want to help. I'll do whatever is necessary to take down the people responsible for our mother's death," Lynn said.

"We need all the help we can get," Dawn said. At that moment a knock sounded on the door.

Kayla jumped up. "That must be Darcy." She opened the door and hugged the woman who stepped in.

Lynn looked at the woman with interest. She knew

from what Kayla and Dawn had told her that Darcy was a former Hollywood makeup artist who now worked as a beautician and a private investigator.

Darcy Steele was fragile looking, with dyed brown hair that she was growing out, judging by the blond roots, and blue eyes. She greeted Dawn with a hug, then turned and smiled at Lynn. "I can see the resemblance," she said, and gestured toward Dawn. "It's amazing. You both have the very same eyes."

For the next couple of minutes it seemed as if everyone was talking at once as the three caught up with each other, and Lynn sat back and watched. She knew from Dawn that Darcy ran a sort of underground railroad for abused women and realized the woman's appearance of fragility hid a wealth of inner strength.

They also told Lynn more about Lab 33, that it was built underground with an entrance in the side of a rock formation. It was Dawn who told her about the many levels of the structure that went down into the earth, and to Lynn it sounded like something from a science-fiction novel. However she knew from the look in Dawn's eyes when she spoke of the place that it was very real and the people who worked there could be very dangerous.

It was a conversation of discovery for Lynn as she learned more about the Athena Academy and the women who had been Rainy's friends.

"You mentioned on the phone that you have news," Kayla said to Darcy.

"I got a late response to the ad," she said.

Lynn looked blankly first at Kayla then at Dawn. It was Dawn who explained. "Darcy has been hunting down the surrogate angle. She found ads in some of the tabloids in the Phoenix area and decided to place an ad of her own."

"I offered a reward for anyone who might have information about surrogate mothers from about twenty years ago. It's through the ad we found Cleo. And now I found somebody else."

"Who?" Kayla asked and leaned forward.

Darcy looked at all of them. "A woman called me. She told me that years ago she worked with a woman who answered an ad for surrogate mothers. She also said that this woman, Tamara Hallwell, paid her to give her a urine sample at the doctor's office. According to the woman who called me, Tamara Hallwell had unusual pale blue eyes. She sounds like a woman Cleo remembered seeing in the doctor's office."

"When Cleo went to the doctor's office for her pregnancy test, she remembered seeing a nervous-looking woman with startling blue eyes," Dawn explained.

"What are you thinking?" Lynn asked. "Why would a woman pay another one for a urine sample?"

"So that nobody would know she was pregnant?" Kayla said.

Darcy nodded and leaned back in her chair. "I'm thinking that maybe this Tamara Hallwell was a third surrogate and she didn't want anyone to know that the pregnancy was a success."

"So she paid a woman who wasn't pregnant to provide a urine sample—and then what happened to her?" Kayla asked.

"She disappeared. Or maybe was killed," Darcy replied. "I've tried to find her and there's no trace."

"If what you're saying is true, then it's possible there's another one of us." Dawn looked at Lynn. "We could have another sister."

Hours later Lynn sat in her motel room alone. The four of them had talked until after ten, then Kayla and Darcy had left to return to their homes, and Dawn and Lynn had gone to separate rooms for the night.

It had been a night of revelations, ending in a new mystery. Someplace there might be another sister, and if that were true then they needed to find her. She and Dawn needed to find the rest of their family.

Family. She got up from the bed and undressed. As she slipped her silk nightgown over her head, she thought of the women she'd met tonight and the rest of the women she knew she'd meet in the future.

Funny, but in a matter of hours she'd felt as though

they were family. She'd felt the bonds that tied them together, bonds of love and respect for each other.

Their obvious love for Rainy Carrington, and their commitment to each other, was as strong a bond as any family could ever offer, and Lynn wallowed in the warmth of knowing that she was now a part of such a warm, caring, strong group of women.

She'd found her place among these women, and she shared their common goal in finding out what had happened so many years before at the Athena Academy and discovering the secrets of Lab 33.

She slid into bed and tried to blank out the neon buzz of the motel sign just outside of her room, the noisy tick of the clock on her nightstand and the sound of water running in another one of the units.

As she quieted the noise of her mind, she heard Nick's deep, sweetly familiar voice telling her that all she needed to do was call him and he'd wait for her.

He hadn't been far from her thoughts throughout the day. Even as she had listened to the women talk about mysteries and potential siblings and danger, Nick had remained in the back of her mind.

She had no idea what the future held. She had no idea where the winds of fate might carry her. She certainly didn't need Nick in her life.

But she wanted him. Eventually, hopefully, the answers they sought would be found, the mysteries all solved and Rainy's children reunited.

It would be nice if she and Nick could pick up the pieces of what they'd only just begun—a relationship that had felt good and right and wonderfully real.

Magic. That's what he'd told her they'd had, a magic they had just begun to explore when she'd had to say goodbye.

She thought of his smile, that slow, sexy grin that warmed her from the inside out. He'd listened to her like no other person had listened in her life. Her opinions and thoughts had been important to him.

He'd asked her to stay, but when she'd made it clear that she had to go, he hadn't tried to change her mind. He'd cared enough about her to let her go. He'd allowed her wings, and she'd known that he hoped eventually those wings would bring her back to him.

She sat on the edge of the bed and stared at the telephone. It was after ten here in New Mexico, which meant it was after midnight in Florida. Too late to call him, she thought, even as her hand reached out for the phone receiver.

She didn't realize she'd memorized his number until she punched it in. She held the receiver tight against her ear as she waited for him to answer.

It was possible that the words he'd spoken to her had been spoken in the heat of the moment, with the adrenaline of Jonas's escape still rushing through him. It was possible now that he no longer needed her to put Jonas behind bars, that he would realize he hadn't meant what he'd said.

If that were the case, she would survive. She had learned in the past couple of days that she could survive many things and, if she had to, she would survive the loss of Nick.

His deep voice filled the line. "Hello?"

She gripped the receiver even tighter, surprised by the depth of emotion that swept through her at the sound of his voice. "Nick? It's me. I know it's late…"

"Lynn. I've been hoping you'd call. Are you okay?"

"I'm fine. I'm not sure why I called."

"Because you miss me?"

She smiled, her heart warming. "Yes, because I miss you."

"I miss you, too."

"Has Jonas been arrested? Did they find him?" This wasn't why she'd called him, wasn't really what she wanted to hear from him.

"So far he's managed to elude us, but that's not important right now. What's important is that you know that my bed isn't the only lonely place right now. My life is lonely without you in it."

She gripped the receiver so tightly she was afraid she might shatter it. This was what she had wanted to hear.

"I don't know any more now than I did this morning. I don't know when I'll be back to Miami or when I'll see you again."

"Lynn, honey, I don't know what demons are chasing you, but you slay them, then you come back to me."

She closed her eyes, her love for him filling her up. "Thank you, Nick. For believing in me."

"I told you, you're an amazing woman. I'm a patient man, Lynnette, when it comes to things that matter to me. You matter. I'll wait."

In those simple words Lynn knew whatever her future held, it definitely included Nick.

* * * * *

Look for the next ATHENA FORCE
adventure, CONTACT by Evelyn Vaughn,
available February 2005
at your favorite retail outlet.

Books by Carla Cassidy

Silhouette Bombshell

Get Blondie #3
Deceived #26

Silhouette Shadows

Swamp Secrets #4
Heart of the Beast #11
Silent Screams #25
Mystery Child #61

Silhouette Intimate Moments

One of the Good Guys #531
Try To Remember #560
Fugitive Father #604
Behind Closed Doors #778
†*Reluctant Wife* #850
†*Reluctant Dad* #856
‡*Her Counterfeit Husband* #885
‡*Code Name: Cowboy* #902
‡*Rodeo Dad* #934
In a Heartbeat #1005
‡*Imminent Danger* #1018
Strangers When We Married #1046
****Man on a Mission* #1077
Born of Passion #1094
****Once Forbidden...* #1115
****To Wed and Protect* #1126
****Out of Exile* #1149
Secrets of a Pregnant Princess #1166
‡‡*Last Seen...* #1233
‡‡*Dead Certain* #1250
‡‡*Trace Evidence* #1261
‡‡*Manhunt* #1294

Silhouette Books

Shadows 1993
"Devil and the Deep Blue Sea"

†Sisters
‡Mustang, Montana
**The Delaney Heirs
‡‡Cherokee Corner

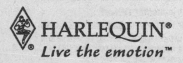

If you enjoyed what you just read,
then we've got an offer you can't resist!

Take 2 bestselling
love stories FREE!

Plus get a FREE surprise gift!

From the forest she will come...

On the trail of Ilduin Bane, a gang of assassin mages whose
blades drip poison and whose minds share a common
purpose, Archer Blackcloak and his band come across
something quite different—a woman named Tess Birdsong.
With no memory, no future and only a white rose to identify
her, Tess joins Archer and his band, bringing with her the will
of one who has nothing to lose.

The road to freedom is long and twisted, but the band
cannot turn back now that they have started—no matter how
high the price to be paid....

On sale January 2005.
Visit your local bookseller.

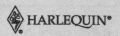

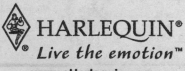

COMING NEXT MONTH

#29 PERSONAL ENEMY—Sylvie Kurtz
When security specialist Adria Caskey's undercover plan to
ruin the man who had destroyed her family went awry, she
found herself protecting the man she loathed most in the
world. But as a cunning stalker drew them into a trap,
her sense of duty battled her desire for revenge....

#30 CONTACT—Evelyn Vaughn
Athena Force
Anonymous police contact Faith Corbett had been a psychic
all her life, but now her undercover work had put her in a serial
killer's sights. As she raced to save innocent lives, she had to
confront the dark secrets about her psychic gift, her family and
the skeptical detective who challenged her at every turn....

#31 THE MEDUSA PROJECT—Cindy Dees
Major Vanessa Blake had the chance to be part of the first
all-female Special Ops team in the U.S. military through
the Medusa Project. Only trouble was, the man charged
with training the women was under orders to make sure
they failed. But when their commander disappeared in
enemy territory, Vanessa and the Medusas were the only
people the government could turn to to retrieve him and
expose a deadly terrorist plot.

#32 THE SPY WORE RED—Wendy Rosnau
Spy Games
When Quest agent Nadja Stefn accepted a mission to
terminate an international assassin and seize his future-kill
files, she had another agenda: finding the child who was
ripped from her at birth. But she hadn't counted on
working with her ex-lover, Bjorn, agent extraordinaire—
and unbeknownst to him, her child's father.